OATH BREAKER

Oath Breaker

Chronicles
of Ancient
Darkness

MICHELLE PAVER

Illustrated by Geoff Taylor

Orion
Children's Books

ORION CHILDREN'S BOOKS

First published in Great Britain in 2008 by Orion Children's Books
This paperback edition first published in 2009 by Orion Children's Books
Reissued in 2011 by Orion Children's Books
This edition published in 2016 by Hodder and Stoughton

16

Text copyright © Michelle Paver, 2008
Illustrations copyright © Geoff Taylor, 2008

The moral rights of the author and illustrator have been asserted.

A CIP catalogue record for this book
is available from the British Library.

ISBN 978 1 84255 116 5

**Printed and bound in Great Britain
by Clays Ltd, Elcograf S.p.A.**

The paper and board used in this book are
made from wood from responsible sources.

MIX
Paper from
responsible sources
FSC® C104740

Orion Children's Books
An imprint of
Hachette Children's Group
Part of Hodder and Stoughton
Carmelite House
50 Victoria Embankment
London EC4Y 0DZ

An Hachette UK Company
www.hachette.co.uk

www.hachettechildrens.co.uk

ONE

Sometimes there's no warning. Nothing at all.

Your skinboat is flying like a cormorant over the waves, your paddle sending silver capelin darting through the kelp, and everything's just right: the choppy Sea, the sun in your eyes, the cold wind at your back. Then a rock rears out of the water, bigger than a whale, and you're heading straight for it, you're going to smash . . .

Torak threw himself sideways and stabbed hard with his paddle. His skinboat lurched – nearly flipped over – and hissed past the rock with a finger to spare.

Streaming wet and coughing up seawater, he struggled to regain his balance.

'You all right?' shouted Bale, circling back.

'Didn't see the rock,' muttered Torak, feeling stupid.

Bale grinned. 'Couple of beginners in camp. You want to

go and join them?'

'You first!' retorted Torak, slapping the water with his paddle and drenching Bale. 'Race you past the Crag!'

The Seal boy gave a whoop and they were off: freezing, wet, exhilarated. High overhead, Torak spotted two black specks. He whistled, and Rip and Rek hurtled down to fly alongside him, their wingtips nearly touching the waves. Torak swerved to avoid a slab of ice and the ravens swerved with him, sunlight glinting purple and green on their glossy black feathers. They edged ahead. Torak raced to keep up. His muscles burned. Salt stung his cheeks. He laughed aloud. This was almost as good as flying.

Bale – two summers older and the best skinboater in the islands – pulled ahead, disappearing into the shadow of the looming headland called the Crag. The Sea turned rougher as they left the bay, and a wave smacked head-on into Torak's boat, nearly upending him.

When he'd got it under control, he was facing the wrong way. The Bay of Seals looked beautiful in the sun, and for a moment he forgot the race. Spray misted the waterfall at the southern end, and gulls wheeled about the cliffs. On the beach, smoke curled from the Seal Clan's humped shelters, and the long racks of salt-rimed cod glittered like frost. He saw Fin-Kedinn, his dark-red hair a fiery beacon among the fairer Seals; and there was Renn, giving an archery lesson to a gaggle of admiring children. Torak grinned. Seals were better with a harpoon than a bow and arrow, and Renn was not a patient teacher.

Bale yelled at him to catch up, so he turned and applied himself to his paddle.

Once past the Crag, they realized they were famished, and put in at a small bay, where they woke up a fire of driftwood and seaweed. Before eating, Bale threw a morsel of dried cod into the shallows for the Sea Mother and his clan guardian, while Torak, who didn't have a guardian, stuck a chunk of elk-blood sausage in a juniper bush as an offering to the Forest. It felt a bit odd, as the Forest was a day's skinboating to the east, but it would have felt even odder not to have done it.

After that, Bale shared the rest of the dried cod – sweet, chewy and surprisingly un-fishy – and Torak pulled clumps of mussels from the rocks. These they ate raw, prising off a half-shell and using it to scrape out the deliciously rich, slippery orange meat. Then Bale helped finish the elk sausage. Like the rest of his clan, he'd become more relaxed about mixing the Forest with the Sea, which made things easier for everyone.

Still hungry, they decided to make a stew. Torak filled his cooking-skin with water from a stream, hung it from sticks beside the fire, and added pebbles which had been heating in the embers. Bale tossed in handfuls of purple sea moss he'd found in a rockpool, and a pile of shellworms he'd dug from the sand, and Torak threw in a bunch of sea kale, because he wanted something green to remind him of the Forest.

As they waited for it to cook, Torak squatted near the fire, scorching the feeling back into his fingers. Bale made a spoon by wedging half a mussel shell in a piece of kelp stem, and binding it with seal sinew from his sewing pouch.

'Good fishing to you!' called a voice from the Sea, making them jump.

It was a Cormorant fisherman in a skinboat. His walrus-hide net bulged with herring.

'And good fishing to you!' Bale returned the greeting

common among the Sea clans.

As he paddled into the shallows, the man peered at Torak, taking in the fine black tattoos on his cheeks. 'Who's your friend from the Forest?' he asked Bale. 'Are those tattoos – Wolf Clan?'

Torak opened his mouth to reply, but Bale got in first. 'He's my kinsman. Fin-Kedinn's foster son. He hunts with the Ravens.'

'And I'm not Wolf Clan,' said Torak. 'I'm clanless.' His stare told the man to make of that what he would.

The man's hand went to the clan-creature feathers on his shoulder. 'I've heard of you. You're the one they cast out.'

Without thinking, Torak touched his forehead, where his headband concealed the outcast tattoo. Fin-Kedinn had altered the tattoo so it no longer meant outcast; but not even the Raven Leader could alter the memory.

'The clans took him back,' said Bale.

'So they say,' said the man. 'Well. Good fishing, then.' He spoke only to Bale, giving Torak a doubtful glance before paddling away.

'Don't mind him,' said Bale after a moment's silence.

Torak didn't reply.

'Here.' Bale tossed him the spoon. 'You left yours in camp. And cheer up! He's a Cormorant. What do they know?'

Torak's lip curled. 'About as much as a Seal.'

Bale lunged for him and they wrestled, laughing, rolling over the pebbles until Torak got Bale in an armlock and made him beg for mercy.

They ate in silence, spitting out scraps for Rip and Rek. Then Torak lay on his side and roasted, and Bale fed the fire with driftwood. The Seal boy didn't notice Rip

4

approaching from behind at a stiff-legged walk. Both ravens were fascinated by Bale's long fair hair, which he wore threaded with blue slate beads and the tiny bones of capelin.

Rip took one of the bones in his powerful bill and tugged. Bale yelped. Rip let go and cowered with half-spread wings: an innocent raven unjustly accused. Bale laughed and tossed him a piece of shellworm.

Torak smiled. It was good to be with Bale again. He was like a brother, or how Torak imagined a brother would be. They enjoyed the same things, laughed at the same jokes. But they were different. Bale was nearly seventeen summers old, and soon he would find a mate and build his own shelter. As the Seals never moved camp, this meant that apart from trading trips to the Forest, he would live out his days on the narrow beach of the Bay of Seals.

Never to move camp. Even thinking of it made Torak breathless and cramped. And yet – to have such certainty. Your whole life unrolling like a well-tanned seal pelt. Sometimes he wondered how that must feel.

Bale sensed the change in him and asked if he was missing the Forest.

Torak shrugged.

'And Wolf?'

'Always.' Wolf had flatly refused to get in a boat, so they'd been forced to leave him behind. *Soon back*, Torak had told his pack-brother in wolf talk. But he wasn't sure if Wolf had understood.

Thinking of Wolf made him restless. 'It's getting late,' he said. 'We need to be on the Crag by dusk.'

That was why he and Renn and Fin-Kedinn had come. The disturbances on the island had started again after the winter, and they suspected it was the Soul-Eaters, searching for the last piece of the fire-opal which had lain hidden since the death of the Seal Mage. For the past half-moon, they'd taken turns to keep watch. Tonight it was the turn of Torak and Bale.

Bale looked preoccupied as he scoured the cooking-skin with sand. He opened his mouth to say something, then shook his head and frowned.

It wasn't like him to hesitate, so it must be important. Torak twisted a frond of oarweed in his fingers and waited.

'When you go back to the Forest,' said Bale without meeting his eyes, 'I'm going to ask Renn to stay here. With me. I want to know what you think about that.'

Torak went very still.

'Torak?'

Torak placed the oarweed on the fire and watched the flames around it turn purple. He felt as if he'd reached the edge of a cliff without knowing it was there. 'Renn can do what she likes,' he said at last.

'But you. What do you think?'

Torak sprang to his feet. Anger made his skin prickle and his heart bump unpleasantly in his chest. He stared down at Bale, who was handsome, older, and part of a clan. He knew that if he stayed, they would fight, and this time it would be for real. 'I'm off,' he said.

'Back to camp?' said Bale, studiedly calm.

'No.'

'Then where?'

'Just off.'

'What about keeping watch?'

'You do it.'

'Torak. Don't be –'

'I said, *you* do it!'

'Right. Right.' Bale stared at the fire.

Torak turned on his heel and ran to his boat.

He headed up the north coast, away from the Bay of Seals. His anger had gone, leaving a cold, churning confusion. He longed for Wolf. But Wolf was far away.

He found another inlet and put in. He carried the skinboat into the straggling trees on the lower slopes, needing the smell of birch and rowan, even if they were stunted and saltblown compared with those of the Forest. He couldn't return to the Bay of Seals, not tonight. He would stay here.

He had no pack or sleeping-sack, but since being cast out, he always carried what he needed wherever he went: axe, knife, tinder pouch. Propping the skinboat upside-down on shoresticks, he stacked branches and last autumn's bracken against the sides to make a shelter. Then he woke a driftwood fire and piled rocks behind it to throw back the heat. There was plenty of dry bracken and seaweed for bedding, and he'd be warm enough in his reindeer-hide parka and leggings. If not, too bad.

It was a clear night at the end of the Birchblood Moon – the Seals called it the Moon of the Cod Run – and from the shallows came the clink of a lonely little ice floe bumping against the rocks. Beyond the firelight, Rip and Rek slept huddled together in the fork of a rowan, their beaks tucked under their wings.

Torak lay watching the flames. It was nine moons since he'd been outcast, but it still felt strange to be in the open and not hiding his fire.

He should go back.

But he couldn't face Bale. Or Fin-Kedinn. Or Renn.

As he hunched deeper into his parka, something dug into his side. It was Bale's spoon; he must have shoved it into his belt before he left. He turned it in his fingers. It was carefully made, the sinew wound tight, the loose end neatly tucked in.

He blew out a long breath. He would go back in the morning and say sorry. Bale would understand. He was good that way, he never sulked.

Torak slept badly. In his dreams he heard an owl calling, and Renn telling him something he didn't understand.

Some time after middle-night, he woke. It was the time of the moon's dark, when it had been eaten by the sky bear, and only a glimmer of starlight rocked on the quiet Sea. He needed to get going: put in at the Bay of Seals, climb the Crag, find Bale.

Feeling groggy and unrested, he dismantled the shelter and poured water on the fire to put it to sleep. Rip and Rek reluctantly stretched their wings and fluffed up their head-feathers to show their dislike of such an early start; but when Torak carried his boat into the shallows and set off, he heard the strong, steady whisper of raven wings.

In the east, the sun was a scarlet knife-slash between Sea and sky, but the Bay of Seals was in shadow, the Crag looming against the stars. The gulls were roosting, the seal-hide shelters silent. Only the waterfall broke the stillness, and the stealthy lapping of the Sea, and the cod creaking on the racks.

Torak came ashore at the north end of the bay. Shells crunched beneath his boots, and he breathed the bitter tang of banked-up fires. On the racks, the cod watched him with dead, salt-crusted eyes.

Rek gave an eager cark – she'd spotted carrion – and both ravens flew to the rocks at the foot of the Crag.

It was too dark for Torak to see what they'd found, but something made the skin on the back of his neck tighten.

Whatever it was, Rip and Rek approached cautiously, as

ravens do, hopping nearer, then flying away.

Torak told himself it could be anything. But he was running, stumbling through mounds of rotting seaweed. As he drew closer, he caught the sickly-sweet smell that is like no other. He sank to his knees.

No. No.

He must have shouted it, because the ravens flew off with caws of alarm.

No.

He crawled closer. His fingers touched wetness and came away red. He saw shards of white bone and spatters of greasy grey sludge. He saw darkness seeping through the long fair hair that was beaded with blue slate and capelin bones. He saw the familiar face staring sightlessly at the sky.

Sometimes there's no warning. Nothing at all.

Two

This isn't happening, thought Torak.

He wasn't staring at those claw-like fingers, at that blood blackening under the nails. It wasn't real.

A gull screamed on the cliff, and Torak raised his head. High above, at the lip of the Crag, a juniper bush hung down. He pictured Bale on his knees, leaning over too far. His desperate grab at a branch, the sickening jolt as it gave way. The rocks hurtling towards him.

Oh, Bale. Why did you go so close to the edge?

A chill wind stole down his neck, and he shivered. Bale's souls were close, and they were angry. Angry with him. *If you'd been with me, I wouldn't have died.*

Torak shut his eyes.

Death Marks. Yes. The souls must be kept together, or Bale might become a demon or a ghost.

At least I can do this for you, thought Torak.

With clumsy fingers, he untied his medicine pouch and shook it. Out fell the medicine horn which had been his mother's, and the little mussel spoon. He blinked. He hadn't even thanked Bale for it. They had eaten in silence. Then they'd fought. No, he corrected himself. Bale didn't fight. *You* did the quarrelling. The last thing you ever said to him was in anger. Death Marks.

He shoved the spoon back into the pouch. Shaking earthblood into his palm, he tried to spit on it, but his mouth was too dry. He stumbled to a rockpool and made the red ochre into a paste with seawater. On his way back, he wound oarweed round his forefinger, so as not to touch the corpse.

Bale lay on his back. His face was unmarked. It was the back of his skull that had cracked like an eggshell. Numbly, Torak daubed earthblood circles on the forehead, chest and heels. He'd done the same for Fa. The mark on Fa's chest had been the hardest, as he had a scar where he'd cut out the Soul-Eater tattoo. Torak's own chest bore a similar scar, so when his time came, that mark would be difficult, too. Bale's chest was smooth. Flawless.

When it was done, Torak sat on his heels. He knew he was too close to the body, that this was the most dangerous time, when the souls are still close, and might try to possess the living. But he stayed where he was.

Someone was crunching through the seaweed, calling his name.

He turned.

Renn saw his face and stopped.

'Stay back.' His voice was rough, as if it belonged to someone else.

She ran to him. She saw what lay beyond. Her cheeks

drained of colour.

'He fell,' said Torak.

She was shaking her head, her lips soundlessly shaping *No, no*. Torak saw her take in the empty gaze, the spattered brains, the blood under the nails. These things would stay with her for ever, and he could do nothing to protect her.

The blood under the nails.

The meaning of it drenched him like an icy wave. That blood wasn't Bale's. Someone else had been with him on the Crag. Bale didn't fall. He was pushed.

Fin-Kedinn appeared behind Renn. His fingers tightened on his staff and his shoulders sagged, but his face remained unreadable. 'Renn,' he said quietly. 'Go and fetch the Seal Clan Leader.'

He had to repeat it twice before she heard, but for once she didn't argue. Like a sleepwalker she trudged towards camp.

Fin-Kedinn turned to Torak. 'How did it happen?'

'I don't know.'

'Why? Weren't you with him?'

Torak flinched. 'No, I . . . I should have been. I wasn't.' *If I'd been with him, he wouldn't have died. This is my fault. My fault.*

Their eyes met, and in Fin-Kedinn's sharp blue gaze, Torak saw understanding and sorrow: sorrow for *him*.

The Raven Leader raised his head and studied the Crag. 'Go up there,' he said. 'Find out who did this.'

The morning sun glinted on the juniper thorns as Torak climbed the steep path towards the Crag. Bale's bootprints were unmistakeable – Torak knew them as well as he knew

Renn's or Fin-Kedinn's or his own – and they were the only ones on the trail. So whoever had killed him hadn't come this way; not from the Seal camp.

Whoever had killed him. It still wasn't real. Only yesterday they'd been gutting cod together on the foreshore; Rip and Rek sidling closer to the steaming entrails, Bale tossing them scraps now and then. At last the final cod hung by its tail from the rack, and they were free to go skinboating. Asrif had lent Torak his boat, and Detlan and his little sister had come to see them off, Detlan on his crutches, waving so hard he nearly fell over.

Only yesterday.

The neck of the Crag was shaggy with rowan and juniper, but from there it broadened into a huge, flat boat shape jutting over the Sea. Long ago, the surface had been traced with a silvery web of hunters and prey. In the middle squatted a grey granite altar shaped like a fish.

Torak swallowed. Two summers before, the Seal Mage had tied him to that altar and prepared to cut out his heart. He could still feel the granite digging into his shoulder blades; still hear the click of the tokoroths' claws.

From far below came a cry like a creature being torn in two. Torak sucked in his breath. Bale's father had found his son.

Don't think about that. Think about this. Do this for Bale.

The Crag glistened with dew. It was naked rock; except for the odd crust of lichen or stonecrop. Tracking would be hard, but if the killer had left any trace, Torak would find it.

From the neck, he scanned the Crag. Something wasn't right, but he couldn't work out what. Storing that for later, he moved forwards. Fa used to say that to track your quarry, you must think yourself into its spirit. This took on a dreadful meaning now. Torak had to see Bale alive on the Crag. He had to see his faceless killer.

The killer must have been strong to have overcome Bale, but that was all Torak knew. He had to make the Crag tell him the rest.

It wasn't long before he found the first sign. He crouched, squinting sideways in the low morning light. A bootprint, very faint. And there: the suggestion of another. An older man walks on his heels, a young man on his toes. Bale had walked lightly onto the Crag.

Step by step, Torak followed him. He forgot the voice of the Sea and the salt wind in his face. He lost himself in the search.

The sense of being watched brought him back. He stopped. His heart began to pound. What if Bale's killer were still hiding in the rowans?

Whipping out his knife, he spun round.

'Torak, it's me!' cried Renn.

With a harsh exhalation, he lowered his knife. '*Never* do that again!'

'I thought you'd heard me!'

'What are you doing here?'

'Same as you!' She was angry because he'd frightened her, but she recovered fast. 'He didn't fall. His finger-nails . . . ' They stared at one another. Torak wondered if he, too, wore that bleak, stretched look.

'How did it happen?' she said. 'I thought you were with him.'

'No.'

She met his eyes. He glanced away. 'You go first,' she said in an altered voice. 'You're the best tracker.'

With his head down, he resumed his search, and Renn

followed. She rarely spoke when he was tracking; she said he went into a kind of trance which she didn't like to break. He was grateful for that now. Sometimes, she saw too much with those dark eyes; and he couldn't tell her about his quarrel with Bale. He was too ashamed.

He hadn't gone far when he found more signs. A crumb of lichen scraped by a running boot; and behind the altar, a lobe of stonecrop ground to a green smear. Snagged in a crack, a strand of reindeer hair. Torak's skin crawled. Bale wore seal hide. This had belonged to his killer. An image began to take shape, like a hunter emerging from mist. A big, heavy man clad in reindeer hide.

At once a name sprang to mind, but Torak pushed it aside. Don't guess. Keep your mind open. Find proof.

He pictured Bale leaving his hiding-place in the rowans, running towards the figure kneeling by the altar. The killer rose. They circled one another, moving closer and closer to the cliff edge.

At one point, the lip of the Crag was cracked, and in the soil the wind had blown in, a juniper clung to life. It had been half yanked out by the roots, and was still oozing tree-blood. Torak saw Bale desperately clutching a branch, his free hand clawing mud. He had fought so hard to live. And the killer had stamped on his fingers.

A red mist descended over Torak's sight. Sweat broke out on his palms. When he caught the killer, he would . . .

'Whoever it was,' said Renn shakily, 'he must have been hugely strong to have beaten B—' she jammed her knuckle in her mouth. For the next five summers, it would be forbidden to speak Bale's name, or else his spirit might return to haunt the living.

'Look there,' said Torak. He picked up a tiny speck of dried spruce-blood. 'And this.' He drew aside a branch to reveal a handprint.

Renn breathed in with a hiss.

Bale's murderer had leaned on one hand to watch his victim fall. That hand had only three fingers.

Torak shut his eyes. He was back in the caves of the Far North, facing the Soul-Eater. Wolf sprang to his defence, leaping at the attacker, snapping off two fingers.

'So now we know,' said Renn in a cold voice.

They stared at one another, both remembering cruel green eyes in a face as hard as cracked earth.

Torak's fist closed over the spruce-blood. 'Thiazzi,' he said.

THREE

The Oak Mage had made no attempt to cover his tracks. He'd found his way down the steep north flank of the Crag to a small pebble beach, picked up his skinboat, and paddled away.

Torak and Renn tracked him to where the trail ended in the Sea.

'From where I was,' said Torak, 'I might have seen him.'

'Why were you camping out here?' said Renn.

'I – I needed to be alone.'

She gave him a penetrating stare, but didn't ask why. That was worse. Maybe she'd guessed that he'd made a terrible mistake; so terrible that she couldn't bring herself to talk of it.

'He might be anywhere by now,' she said, turning back to the waves. 'He could've made for the Kelp Island, or one of the smaller ones. Or gone back to the Forest.'

'And he's got a head start,' said Torak. 'Let's go.'

To return to the Seal camp, they had to climb all the way to the Crag again. The altar still looked subtly wrong. It was Renn who noticed why. 'The carvings. The tip of the altar is lying across that elk's head. That can't be right.'

'It's been moved.' Torak was appalled that he hadn't seen it sooner. The scrape marks were as plain as a raven on an ice floe. He pictured the Oak Mage – the strongest man in the Forest – putting his shoulder to the altar to shift it, then moving it back, but leaving it just out of true.

Under the tip of the altar, Torak found what Thiazzi had uncovered: a small hollow hacked from the surface of the Crag. It was empty.

'He found what he was after,' said Torak.

Neither of them voiced their fear. But among the rowans on the neck, Torak found proof: the remains of a little pouch of dehaired seal hide. The crumbling hide still bore the faint imprint of something hard, about the size of a sloe, which had nestled inside.

Torak's blood thudded in his ears. Renn's voice reached him from a great distance. 'He found it, Torak. Thiazzi has the fire-opal.'

'Tell no-one,' said Fin-Kedinn. 'Not that he was murdered, or who did it, or why.'

Torak agreed at once, but Renn was aghast. 'Not even his father?'

'No-one,' said the Raven Leader.

They squatted by the stream at the south end of the bay, daubing each other's faces with clay mourning marks. The

18

roar of the waterfall drowned their voices. There was no danger of being overheard by the Seal women downstream who were preparing the funeral feast, or by the men readying Bale's skinboat for the Death Journey. The Seals worked in silence to avoid offending the dead boy's souls. Torak thought they seemed like people in a dream.

All day, they had worked, and he had helped. Now dusk was falling, and every shelter, every skinboat, every last rack of cod had been moved to this end of the bay, furthest from the Crag. To the north, only the shelter Bale had shared with his father remained. It had been doused in seal oil and set ablaze. Torak could see it: a red eye glaring at him in the gathering dark.

'But that's *wrong*,' protested Renn.

'It's necessary.' Her uncle caught her gaze and held it. 'Think, Renn. If his father knew, he'd seek revenge.'

'Yes, and so?' she retorted.

'He wouldn't be alone,' said Fin-Kedinn. 'The whole clan would want to avenge one of their own.'

'So?' repeated Renn.

'I know Thiazzi,' said Fin-Kedinn. 'He won't hide in the islands, he'll head back to the Forest, where his power is greatest. The quickest route takes him past the trading meet on the coast . . .'

'And if the Seals came after him,' put in Torak, 'he'd set them against the other clans and get away.'

The Raven Leader nodded. 'That's why we say nothing. The Sea clans and the Forest clans have never been on easy terms. Thiazzi would use that. That's his strength, he fosters hate. Promise me, both of you. Tell no-one.'

'I promise,' said Torak. He didn't want the Seals going after Thiazzi. Revenge must be his and his alone.

Reluctantly, Renn gave her word. 'But his father's bound to find out,' she said. 'He must have seen what we saw. The – the blood under his nails.'

'No,' said Fin-Kedinn. 'I saw to it.' With the grey bars across his brow and down his cheeks, he looked remote and forbidding. 'Come,' he said, rising to his feet. 'It's time we joined the others.'

On the shore, the Seals had set a ring of kelp torches: a leaping orange beneath the dark-blue sky. Within this, they had laid Bale in his skinboat. Greasy black smoke stung Torak's eyes, and he breathed the stink of burning seal oil. He felt the mourning marks stiffening on his skin.

He thought, Bale's funeral rites. This can't be.

First, Bale's father stepped towards the boat and gently covered the body with his sleeping-sack. He had lost both his sons to the Soul-Eaters, and his face was distant, as if he weren't experiencing any of this. As if, thought Torak, he was at the bottom of the Sea.

After him, every member of the clan added a gift for the Death Journey. Asrif gave a food bowl, Detlan a set of fishing-hooks, while his little sister – who'd been very keen on Bale – managed to keep from crying for long enough to put in a small stone lamp. Others gave clothes, dried whale meat or cod, seal nets, spears, rope. Fin-Kedinn gave a harpoon, Renn her three best arrows. Torak gave his pike-jaw amulet, for hunting luck.

Standing to one side, he watched the men raise the skinboat on their shoulders and carry it down to the shallows. There they lashed two heavy stones to prow and stern, and Bale's father got in his own skinboat and began towing his son out to Sea.

The others trudged back for the silent feast, but Torak remained, watching the skinboats dwindle to specks.

When they were out of sight of land, Bale's father would take his spear and gash the funeral boat, sending his son down to the Sea Mother. The fishes would eat Bale's flesh, as in life he had eaten theirs; and when his shelter was ashes and the ashes had blown away, all trace of him would be gone, like a ripple on the Sea.

But he'll come back, thought Torak. He was born here. This was his home. He'll be lonely at Sea.

Fin-Kedinn was speaking his name. 'Torak. Come. You must join the feast.'

'I can't,' he said without turning round.

'You must.'

'I can't! I have to go after Thiazzi.'

'Torak, it's dark,' said Renn at her uncle's side, 'and there's no moon, you can't leave now. We'll set off first thing in the morning.'

'You must honour your kinsman,' Fin-Kedinn said severely.

Torak turned on him. 'My kinsman? That's what we've got to call him, isn't it? My kinsman. The Seal Clan boy. For five whole summers, till we've forgotten his name.'

'We'll never forget,' said Fin-Kedinn. 'But it's better this way. You know that.'

'Bale,' said Torak, very distinctly. 'His name. Was Bale.'

Renn gasped.

Fin-Kedinn watched him narrowly.

'Bale,' said Torak again. 'Bale. Bale. Bale!'

Shouldering past them, he ran the length of the bay, only stopping when he reached the smouldering ruins of Bale's shelter.

'*Bale!*' he shouted at the cold Sea. And if that summoned Bale's vengeful spirit to haunt him, then let it. It was *his* fault that Bale lay at the bottom of the Sea. If he hadn't quarrelled, Bale would not have been alone on the Crag. They would have faced the Oak Mage together, and Bale would still be alive.

His fault.

'Torak!'

Renn stood on the other side of the fire, her pale face shimmering in the heat. 'Stop naming him! You'll draw his spirit!'

'Let it come!' he flung back. 'It's only what I deserve!'

'You didn't kill him, Torak.'

'But it was *my* fault! How do I bear it?'

To that she had no answer.

'Fin-Kedinn's right!' he cried. 'The Seals can't avenge Bale, that's for *me* to do!'

'Don't keep naming him –'

'Vengeance is *mine*!' he shouted. Drawing his knife and taking his medicine horn from its pouch, he raised them to the sky. 'I swear to you, Bale. I swear to you on this knife and this horn and on my three souls – I will hunt the Oak Mage and I will kill him. I *will* avenge you!'

FOUR

Wolf stands in the Bright Soft Cold at the foot of the Mountain, gazing up at Darkfur.

She is many lopes above him, gazing down. He catches her scent, he hears the wind whispering through her beautiful black fur. He lashes his tail and whines.

Darkfur wags her tail and whines back. But this is the Thunderer's Mountain. Wolf can't go up, and she can't come down.

All through the Long Cold he has missed her, even when he was hunting with Tall Tailless and the pack-sister, or playing hunt-the-lemming, especially then, because Darkfur is so good at it. Of all the wolves in the Mountain pack, Wolf misses her the most. They are one breath, one bone. He feels this in his fur.

Darkfur goes down on her forepaws and barks. *Come! The*

hunt is good, the pack is strong!

Wolf's tail droops.

Her bark becomes impatient.

I cannot! he tells her.

With a leap, she is bounding down the Mountain. The Bright Soft Cold flies from her paws as she races towards him, and Wolf's heart flies with it. Joyfully he lopes towards her, running so fast that he . . .

Wolf woke up.

He was out of the Now that he went to in his sleeps, and back in the other now, lying at the edge of the Great Wet. Alone. He missed Darkfur. He missed Tall Tailless and the pack-sister. He even missed the ravens, a bit. *Why* did Tall Tailless leave him and go off in the floating hides?

Wolf hated it here. The sharp earth bit his pads, and the fish-birds attacked if he got too close to their nests. For a while, he'd explored the Dens of the taillesses along the Great Wet, and the Fast Wet that ran into it, but now he was bored.

The taillesses didn't hunt, they just stood around yipping and yowling and staring at stones. They seemed to think that some stones mattered more than others, although they all smelt the same to Wolf; and when the taillesses gave each other stones, they quarrelled. When a normal wolf gives a present – a bone or an interesting stick – he does it because he likes the other wolf, not because he's cross.

The Dark came, and the taillesses settled down for their endless sleep. Wolf heaved himself up and went to nose around the Dens. Scornfully evading the dogs, he ate some fishes hanging from sticks, and a delicious hunk of fish-dog fat. Then he found an overpaw outside a Den and ate that too. When the Light came, he trotted into the

Forest, trod down some bracken to make a comfortable sleeping-patch, and had a nap.

The smell woke him instantly.

His claws tightened. His hackles rose. He knew that smell. It made him remember bad things. It made the tip of his tail hurt.

The scent trail was strong, and it led up-Wet. With a growl, Wolf leapt to his feet and raced after it.

'I told you,' said the Sea-eagle hunter, tying up a bundle of roe buck antlers. 'I saw a big man coming ashore. That's it.'

'Where did he go?' said Torak. He was relentless. Renn, cradling a cup of hot birch-blood in her hands, wondered how much more the Sea-eagle would take.

'I don't *know*!' snapped the hunter. 'I was busy, I wanted to trade!'

'I think he went upriver,' said the hunter's mate.

'Upriver,' repeated Torak.

'That could mean anywhere,' said Renn. But already Torak was heading for the Raven camp and the deerhide canoes.

It was the second night after Bale's funeral rites, and after an exhausting crossing, they'd reached the trading meet on the coast. Fog shrouded the camps along the shore and the mouth of the Elk River. Willow, Sea-eagle, Kelp, Raven, Cormorant, Viper: all had come to barter horn and antler for seal hide and flint Sea eggs. Fin-Kedinn had gone to return their borrowed skinboats to the Whale Clan, and the ravens were roosting in a pine tree. There was no sign of Wolf.

Renn ran to catch up with Torak, who was shouldering

through the throng, earning irritable glances, which he ignored. 'Torak, wait!' Glancing round to make sure they weren't overheard, she said in a low voice, 'Have you thought that this could be a trap? The Soul-Eaters have set traps for you before.'

'I don't care,' said Torak.

'But think! Somewhere out there are Thiazzi and Eostra: the two remaining Soul-Eaters, and the most powerful of all.'

'I don't *care*! He killed my kinsman. I'm going to kill him. And *don't* tell me to get some sleep and we'll start in the morning.'

'I wasn't going to,' she replied, nettled. 'I was going to say I'll fetch some supplies.'

'No time. He's already got two days' lead.'

'And it'll be more,' she retorted, 'if we have to keep stopping to hunt!'

When she reached the shelter she shared with Saeunn, the sight of its familiar, lumpy reindeer hides brought her to a halt. Less than a moon ago, she'd left it and run down to the skinboats, eager to have Fin-Kedinn and Torak to herself, and to see Bale again.

She shut her eyes. In disbelief, she had stared at his broken body. The blind blue gaze. The grey sludge on the rocks. Those are his thoughts, she'd told herself. His thoughts soaking into the lichen.

Night and day, she saw it. She didn't know if Torak did too, because if he talked at all, it was about finding Thiazzi. He didn't seem to have anything left for grief.

Fog trickled down her neck, and she shivered. She was tired and stiff from the crossing, and hollow with grief, and *lonely*. She hadn't known she could be so lonely among people she loved.

Around her, hunters appeared and disappeared in the murk. She thought of Thiazzi gloating over the fire-opal. A man who took pleasure in others' pain. Who lived only to rule.

The Raven Mage huddled in her corner beneath a musty elk pelt. Over the winter, she had shrunk in upon herself till she reminded Renn of an empty waterskin. She rarely hobbled further than the midden, and when the clan moved camp, they carried her on a litter. Renn wondered what kept that shrivelled heart beating, and for how much longer. Already, Saeunn's breath carried a whiff of the Raven bone-grounds.

Trying not to wake her, Renn gathered her gear and crammed supplies into auroch-gut bags. Baked hazelnuts, smoked horse meat, meal of pounded silverweed root; dried lingonberries for Wolf.

The elk pelt stirred.

Renn's heart sank.

The speckled pate emerged from the fur, and the flinty eyes of the Raven Mage regarded her. 'So,' said Saeunn in a voice like the rattle of dead leaves. 'You're leaving. You must know where he's gone.'

'No,' said Renn. Saeunn could always place her talon on a weakness.

'But the Forest is vast . . . You must have tried to see where he went.'

She meant Magecraft. Renn's hands tightened on the gutskin. 'No,' she muttered.

'Why?'

'I couldn't.'

'But you have the skill.'

'No. I don't.' Suddenly, she was close to tears. 'I'm supposed to see the future,' she said bitterly, 'but I couldn't

27

foresee his death. What's the *good* of being a Mage if I couldn't foresee that?'

'You might be able to do Magecraft,' rasped Saeunn, 'but you're not yet a Mage.'

Renn blinked.

'You'll know it when you are. Though perhaps your tongue will know before you do.'

Riddles, thought Renn savagely. Why always riddles?

'Yes, riddles,' said Saeunn with a wheeze that was almost a laugh. 'Riddles for you to solve!' She paused to catch her breath. 'I've been casting the bones.'

Torak appeared in the doorway and threw Renn an impatient glance.

She motioned him to silence. 'What did you see?' she asked Saeunn.

The Mage licked her gums with a tongue as grey as mould. 'A scarlet tree. An ash-haired hunter burning inside. Demons. Scrabbling under scorched stones.'

'Did you see where Thiazzi went?' Torak said brusquely.

'Oh, yes . . . I saw.'

Fin-Kedinn appeared beside Torak, his face grim. 'He's heading for the Deep Forest.'

'The Deep Forest,' echoed Saeunn. 'Yes . . . '

'A group of Boar just arrived,' said Fin-Kedinn. 'They came down the Widewater. At the ford, they saw a big man in a dugout, heading up the Blackwater.'

Torak nodded. 'He's Oak Clan, that's Deep Forest. Of course, that's where he'll go.'

'We'll take two canoes,' said Fin-Kedinn. 'I've told the clan they're to stay here while we head upriver.'

'*We?*' Torak said sharply.

'I'm coming with you,' said Fin-Kedinn.

'So am I,' said Renn, but they ignored her.

'Why?' Torak asked Fin-Kedinn. With a pang, Renn saw that he didn't want them. He wanted to do this on his own.

'I know the Deep Forest,' said Fin-Kedinn. 'You don't.'

'No!' Saeunn was fierce. 'Fin-Kedinn. You must not go!'

They stared at her.

'One thing more the bones revealed, and this is *certain*. Fin-Kedinn, you will not reach the Deep Forest.'

Renn's heart clenched. 'Then – we'll go without him. Just Torak and me.'

But her uncle wore the expression she dreaded: the one which told her there was no point in arguing. 'No, Renn,' he said with terrifying calm. 'You can't do this without me.'

'Yes we can,' she insisted.

Fin-Kedinn sighed. 'You know there's been trouble between the Aurochs and the Forest Horses since last summer. They won't let in outsiders. But they know me –'

'No!' cried Renn. 'Saeunn means it. She's never wrong.'

The Raven Mage shook her head and gave another rattling sigh. 'Ah, Fin-Kedinn . . .'

'Torak, tell him!' pleaded Renn. 'Tell him we can do it without him.'

But Torak picked up a bag of supplies and avoided her eyes. 'Come on,' he muttered, 'we're losing time.'

Fin-Kedinn took the other bag from her hands. 'Let's go,' he said.

FIVE

Wolf raced after the scent trail.

Around him the Forest was waking from its long sleep, and the prey was thin from scraping away the Bright Soft Cold to get at its food. Wolf startled an elk nibbling a sycamore's juicy hide. A herd of reindeer sensed he wasn't hunting them, and raised their heads to watch him pass.

The hated scent streamed over his nose. Many Lights and Darks ago, the bad tailless had trapped him in a tiny stone Den and bound his muzzle so that he couldn't howl. The bad tailless had starved him and stamped on his tail, and when Wolf yelped in pain, he'd *laughed*. Then he'd attacked Wolf's pack-brother. Wolf had leapt at the bad tailless, clamping his jaws on one hairy forepaw, crunching bones and rich, juicy flesh.

Wolf loped faster. He didn't know *why* he sought the

Bitten One – wolves do not hunt taillesses, not even bad ones – but he knew that he had to follow.

The scent thickened. Through the voices of wind and birch and bird, Wolf heard the tailless stirring the Wet with a stick. He smelt that the tailless had no dog.

Then he saw him.

The Bitten One was sliding up-Wet on the trunk of an oak. Wolf caught the glint of a great stone claw at his flank. He caught the smell of pine-blood and reindeer hide, and of the strange, terrible Bright Beast-that-Bites-Cold.

Terror seized Wolf in its jaws. The Bitten One sat fearless, relishing his strength. He was very, very strong. Not even the Bright Beast-that-Bites-Hot dared attack him. Wolf knew this because he'd seen the tailless thrust his forepaw *right into the muzzle of the Bright Beast* – and take it out unbitten.

From many lopes away came the high, thin howl of the bird bone that Tall Tailless and the pack-sister used for calling him.

Wolf didn't know what to do. He longed to go to them; but that would mean turning back.

The bird bone went on calling.

The Bitten One went on sliding up-Wet.

Wolf didn't know what to do.

'You let him get away!' shouted Torak, so angry that he forgot to talk wolf. 'He was right there and you let him get away!'

Wolf tucked his tail between his legs and shot behind Fin-Kedinn, who was on his knees, waking a fire.

'Torak, stop it!' cried Renn.

'But he was so close!'

'I know, but it's not his fault. It was me!'

He turned on her.

'*I* called Wolf,' she told him. 'It's my fault he let Thiazzi get away.' She opened her palm, and he saw the little grouse-bone whistle he'd given her two summers before.

'*Why?*' he demanded.

'I was worried about him. And you – you didn't seem to care.'

That made him even angrier. 'Of course I care! How could I not care about Wolf?'

Behind Fin-Kedinn, Wolf dropped his ears and doubtfully wagged his tail.

Remorse broke over Torak. What was wrong with him?

Wolf had bounded so joyfully into camp, proudly telling Torak how he'd left the trail of the Bitten One as soon as he'd heard his call. He'd been bewildered when Torak lost his temper. He had no idea what he'd done wrong.

Torak sank to his knees and grunt-whined. Wolf raced towards him. Torak buried his face in his scruff. *Sorry.* Wolf licked his ear. *I know.*

'What's wrong with me?' murmured Torak.

Fin-Kedinn, who'd ignored his outburst, told him to go and fetch water. Renn simply glared.

Torak grabbed the waterskin and ran to the shallows.

They'd spent the night and next morning heading up the Elk River, pausing only for brief rests, and were now close to the rapids where the Widewater and the Blackwater crashed together. Twice they'd met hunters who'd seen a big man heading upstream.

He's getting away, thought Torak. Slumping onto a log,

he glowered at the river.

It was a blustery day and the Forest was at odds with itself. An abandoned elk bellowed mournfully. In the dead reeds on the other side, two hares battered each other with their forepaws.

Torak caught the scent of woodsmoke and an appetizing sizzle of flatcakes. He was hungry, but he couldn't join the others. He felt cut off from them, as if he were trapped behind a wall: unseen, but tough as midwinter ice. Saeunn's prophesy about his foster father haunted him. What if Renn was right, and Thiazzi was setting a trap? What if he, Torak, were leading Fin-Kedinn to his death?

And yet – he had no choice but to go on.

Wolf padded down the bank and dropped a stick at Torak's feet as a present.

Torak picked it up and turned it in his fingers.

You're sad, said Wolf with a twitch of one ear. *Why?*

The pale-pelt who smells of fish-dog, Torak said in wolf talk. *Not-Breath. Killed by the Bitten One.*

Wolf rubbed his flank against Torak's shoulder, and Torak leaned against him, feeling his solid, furry warmth.

You hunt the Bitten One, said Wolf.

Yes, said Torak.

Because he is bad?

– because he killed my pack-brother.

Wolf watched a damselfly skim the water. *And when the Bitten One is Not-Breath – does the pale-pelt breathe again?*

No, said Torak.

Wolf tilted his head and looked at Torak, his amber eyes puzzled. *Then – why?*

Because, Torak wanted to tell him, I have to avenge Bale. But he didn't know how to say that in wolf talk, and even if

33

he could, he didn't think Wolf would understand. Maybe wolves didn't seek revenge.

Side by side, they sat watching the midges darting over the brown water. Torak caught the flicker of a trout, and followed it deeper.

He'd always known there were differences between him and Wolf; but Wolf couldn't seem to grasp that. At times it made Wolf frustrated, especially when Torak couldn't do everything a real wolf could. Thinking of this made Torak sad, and vaguely uneasy.

He looked round to find that Wolf had gone, and clouds had darkened the sky. Someone stood in the reeds on the other side of the river, staring at him.

It was Bale.

Water ran soundlessly from his jerkin. Seaweed clotted his streaming hair. His face had a greenish underwater pallor, and his eyes were dark as bruises. Angry. Accusing.

Torak tried to cry out. He couldn't. His tongue had stuck to the roof of his mouth.

Bale raised one dripping arm and pointed at him. His lips moved. No sound came, but his meaning was clear. *Your fault.*

'Torak?'

The spell broke. Torak jerked round.

'I've been calling you!' said Renn, standing behind him, looking cross.

Bale was gone. Across the river, dead reeds creaked in the breeze.

'What's wrong?' said Renn.

'N-nothing,' he faltered.

'*Nothing?* You're as grey as ash.'

He shook his head. He couldn't bring himself to tell her. She gave a small, hurt shrug. 'Well. I saved you a flatcake.' She held it out, wrapped in a dock leaf to keep warm. 'You can eat it as we go.'

From the canoe, Renn watched Wolf running between the trees: now lifting his muzzle to catch the scent, now snuffling in the brush.

Too many times, he'd found the places where the Oak Mage had stopped to eat or camp. Thiazzi seemed in no hurry to reach the Deep Forest, and this worried Renn, although she hadn't mentioned it to the others. Fin-Kedinn was preoccupied, while Torak . . .

She wished he would turn and talk to her. He sat in front, his back straight and unyielding as he searched the banks for signs of Thiazzi.

Angrily, she dug in her paddle. He didn't care about anything except finding the Oak Mage. He didn't even care that Fin-Kedinn was in danger.

At last they reached the rapids, and went ashore to carry the canoes around them. Wolf was already trotting purposefully up the Blackwater.

'How far to the Deep Forest?' asked Torak as they set down the second canoe.

'A day,' said the Raven Leader, 'maybe more.'

Torak ground his teeth. 'If he reaches it, we'll never find him.'

'We might,' said Fin-Kedinn. 'He's taking his time.'

'I wish we knew why,' said Renn. 'Maybe it *is* a trap. And even if it isn't, he'll soon know he's being hunted.'

Fin-Kedinn nodded, but did not reply. All day he'd been distant and uncommunicative, and every so often he narrowed his eyes, as if the Blackwater revived memories that cut too deep.

Renn didn't like it, either. She didn't know this river, as Fin-Kedinn had never led the Ravens to camp on its banks, but she thought it was well-named. It was shadowed by dank trees, and so murky that she couldn't see the bottom. When she leaned over, it gave off a sour smell of rotting leaves.

Once they had the canoes in the water again, she insisted on sitting in front. She was sick of staring at Torak's back, wondering what he was thinking. No doubt it was about finding Thiazzi. Although what, she wondered, would he do if he did? Clan law forbade killing a man without warning, so he'd have to challenge the Oak Mage to a fight. Her mind shied away from that. Torak was strong and quite good at fighting, but he wasn't yet fifteen summers old. How could he challenge the strongest man in the Forest?

'Renn?' he said, making her jump.

She twisted round.

'When someone's asleep, can you tell if they're dreaming? I mean, by watching them?'

She stared at him. His mouth was set, and he avoided her gaze. 'If you're dreaming,' she told him, 'your eyes move. That's what Saeunn says.'

He nodded. 'If you see me dreaming, will you wake me up?'

'Why? Torak, what did you see?'

He shook his head. He was like a wolf; if he didn't want to do something, it was impossible to make him.

She tried anyway. 'What *is* it? Why can't you tell me?'

He opened his mouth, and for a moment she thought he would. Then his eyes widened and he grabbed her hood, yanking her down so hard that she bashed her temple on the rim of the canoe.

'Ow!' she yelled. 'What are you – '

'Fin-Kedinn, get down!' shouted Torak at the same time.

As Renn struggled to right herself, something hissed over her head. She saw Fin-Kedinn reach for his knife and slash; she saw Wolf yelp as if stung by a hornet and leap into the air. She saw a line as thin as a thread of gossamer snap and trail harmlessly in the water.

There was a breathless silence. Renn sat up, rubbing her temple. Torak steered the canoe into midstream and caught the end of the line. 'It was taut as a bowstring,' he said.

He didn't need to say more. Canoes powering towards a strong line of sinew stretched between trees on opposite banks. At head height.

Renn's hand went to her neck. If Torak hadn't pulled her down, it would have cut her throat.

'He knows he's being hunted,' said Fin-Kedinn, bringing his canoe alongside theirs.

'But – maybe he doesn't know it's Torak,' said Renn.

'Why do you say that?' said Torak.

'If he knew it was you,' she said, 'would he risk killing you? He wants your power.'

'Maybe, maybe not,' said Fin-Kedinn. 'Thiazzi is arrogant. Above all things, he believes in his own strength. And he has the fire-opal. He may not think he needs the power of the spirit walker. And if that's right,' he added, 'it means he doesn't care who he kills.'

SIX

The sinew had cut across Wolf's foreleg. It was scarcely bleeding and he wasn't in pain, but Torak insisted on rubbing in a salve of yarrow leaves in marrowfat which he made Renn produce from her medicine pouch.

'He'll only lick it off,' she told him, and Wolf immediately did.

Torak didn't care. It made him feel a bit better, even if it didn't do much for Wolf.

He'd nearly missed that sinew. What if he had, and Renn or Fin-Kedinn had suffered for his mistake? The mere thought made his belly turn over. It only takes one mistake, just one, and you've got to live with the consequences for the rest of your life.

Squatting on the bank, he mashed a handful of wet soapwort to a green froth, and washed his hands.

He glanced up to find Fin-Kedinn watching him. They were alone. Wolf was drinking in the shallows, and Renn was already in the canoe.

Fin-Kedinn emptied the waterskin over Torak's hands. 'Don't worry about me,' he said.

'But I do,' said Torak. 'Saeunn meant what she said.'

The Raven Leader shrugged. 'Omens. You can't live your life by what *might* happen.' He shouldered the waterskin. 'Let's go.'

They followed Wolf up the Blackwater until long into the night, then slept under the canoes, and headed off before dawn. As the afternoon wore on, the Forest closed in. Wakeful spruce thronged the banks, dripping with beard-moss, and even the trees not yet in leaf were vigilant. Last autumn's oak leaves rattled in the wind, and ash buds glinted like tiny black spears.

At last, the hills bordering the Deep Forest rose into view. Torak had reached them two summers before, but then he'd been further north. Here they were steeper, stonier: sheer walls of grey rock, hacked and slashed as if by a giant axe. The hammering cries of black grouse echoed like falling stones.

As the light began to fail, Wolf leapt into the river and swam across. Once on the north bank, he gave himself a good shake, and set off. Then he doubled back, snuffing the mud.

They edged into the shallows, and Torak got out to examine the mess of tracks. No wonder Wolf was puzzled: they were almost unreadable, as a boar had recently taken a wallow.

'This isn't only Thiazzi,' said Torak. 'See that heel print? It's not as heavy, and the weight's more to the inside of the foot.'

'So someone was with him?' said Renn.

He chewed his thumbnail. 'No. Thiazzi's tracks are darker, and a beetle crawled over the other's but not over his. Whoever it was, they came before.'

Wolf had smelt something. Leaving the canoes, they went after him, into a gully cut by a stream feeding into the Blackwater.

Twenty paces up, Torak stopped.

The footprint shouted at him from the mud. Bold, mocking. *Here I am*. Thiazzi stamping his mark for all to see.

'The Oak Mage,' said Fin-Kedinn.

It told Torak a lot more than that. A single footprint is a landscape which can tell a whole story if you know how to read it. Torak did. And before leaving the Seal Island, he'd studied Thiazzi's tracks till he knew every detail.

He found more. He made the gully reveal its secrets. 'He left his dugout in the shallows,' he said at last, 'then climbed up here. He was carrying something heavy on his left shoulder, maybe his axe. Then he retraced his steps, got into his dugout, paddled away.' He clenched his fists. 'He's well fed and rested, moving fast. He's enjoying this.'

'But why come here?' said Renn, looking about her.

'I don't like it,' said Fin-Kedinn. 'Remember that sinew. Let's go back to the boats.'

'No,' said Torak. 'I want to know what he was doing.'

Fin-Kedinn sighed. 'Don't get too far ahead.'

Warily, they advanced: Torak and Wolf first, then Renn, with Fin-Kedinn at the rear.

The trees thinned, and Torak clambered between massive, tumbled boulders, while Wolf bounded lightly ahead. The trail veered to the right. The trees ended.

Torak found himself on a huge, desolate hill of bare

rock. A hundred paces above, the crown was streaked black, as if by fire. Before him, the slope was a chaos of fallen trees thrown there by a flood, with boulders jutting through like broken teeth. Below, the Blackwater coiled round the base of the hill and disappeared between two towering rocks that leaned crazily towards each other. Beyond these great stone jaws rose the looming oaks and jagged spruce of the Deep Forest.

Wolf pricked his ears. Uff! he barked softly.

Torak followed his gaze. Under the willows overhanging the river, he saw the flash of a paddle.

Wolf bounded down the slope. Torak ran after him, nearly losing his footing as a tree-trunk shifted under his boot.

'Torak!' Renn whispered behind him.

'Slow down!' warned Fin-Kedinn.

Torak ignored them. He couldn't let his quarry escape now.

Suddenly there he was, not fifty paces away: driving the dugout with long, powerful strokes towards the Deep Forest.

Wobbling and lurching over the fallen trees, Torak pulled an arrow from his quiver and nocked it to his bow. He no longer heard the others. All he heard was the splash of Thiazzi's paddle, all he saw was that long russet hair lifting in the breeze. He forgot clan law, he forgot everything except the need for revenge.

A log rolled beneath him. Something snagged his ankle. He kicked himself free. Behind him, a loud snap. He glanced round. In one frozen heartbeat he took in the trip-line lashed to the trigger log, its end sharpened to a point and smeared with mud to hide the fresh-cut wood.

The hill of logs began to move. *You fool. Another trap.*

Then the logs were crashing towards him and he was yelling a warning to the others and leaping for the nearest boulder, flinging himself into the tiny hollow beneath it; and logs were bouncing over him, smashing into the river, sending up plumes of water. Huddled under his boulder, Torak heard laughter echo from hill to hill. He pictured Thiazzi's dugout sweeping between the great stone jaws, disappearing into the Deep Forest.

Then the whole hillside was giving way, and Fin-Kedinn was shouting, 'Renn! *Renn!*'

SEVEN

Silence boomed in Torak's ears. Dust clogged his throat.
'Renn?' he called.

No answer.

'Fin-Kedinn? Wolf?'

The rocks threw back the sound of his terror.

He was squashed under a tangle of saplings which had
fallen on top of his boulder. A surge of panic. He was
trapped. Wildly, he struggled. The saplings shifted. He
pushed his way out and greedily gulped air.

'Renn!' he shouted. 'Fin-Kedinn!'

Wolf appeared on the crown of the hill and ran down to
him, his claws clicking on rock. Torak didn't need to say
anything. A terse nose-nudge, and they began to search.
Tree-trunks shifted and creaked ominously. Someone was
whimpering. 'No no, not them, please not them.' It took

Torak a moment to recognize the voice as his own.

A flurry of wings, and Rek lit onto a branch ten paces away. Wolf raced towards her and barked. Torak wobbled after them.

Through the branches he saw a shock of dark-red hair. 'Renn?'

He tore at the branches, dragged saplings out of the way. Thrusting his arm through a gap, he grabbed her sleeve.

She moaned.

'You all right?'

She coughed. Mumbled something that might have been yes.

'There's a gap, I'll make it bigger. Give me your hand, I'll pull you through.' Being Renn, she pushed her bow through first – then wriggled out. Her eyes were huge, but apart from scratches, she was unhurt.

'Fin-Kedinn,' she said.

'I can't find him.'

The blood drained from her face. 'He saved my life. Threw me out of the way.'

Wolf stood below them in a wreck of dead spruce, looking down between his forepaws. His ears were pricked. Eagerly he glanced at his pack-brother.

The spruce lay on top of a larger beech, itself aslant more spruce. Under the beech lay Fin-Kedinn.

'Fin-Kedinn?' Renn's voice shook. *'Fin-Kedinn!'*

The Raven Leader's eyes remained closed.

Frantically, they tugged at branches and tree-trunks. There was a creak, and the whole pile shuddered. They didn't speak, for fear of bringing down disaster.

The sun set, and they worked on. At last they cleared a way to the beech. It wouldn't budge. Torak wedged a sapling underneath and pushed with all his might. The beech shifted slightly.

'We'll have to drag him out,' said Renn.

It took both of them to haul him free. Still he didn't move. Renn held her wrist to his lips to feel for breath. Torak saw her throat work.

Half-carrying, half-dragging him, they finally made it to solid rock. On the hill's eastern flank, facing the Deep Forest, Torak found an overhang. The ledge beneath it was big enough to shelter them, although not high enough to stand up in.

Renn knelt beside her uncle, twisting her hands. Rip and Rek flapped their wings and cawed. Wolf sniffed the Raven Leader's temple. Then he whined, so high that Torak could hardly hear. He went on whining.

Fin-Kedinn's eyelids flickered. 'Where's Renn?' he murmured.

By taking the weight of the other trees, the beech had saved his life, but it had crushed the left side of his chest.

Renn set to work, pulling off his parka and cutting the laces on his jerkin. She was as gentle as she could be, but the pain was so bad that he nearly passed out.

'Three ribs broken,' she said as she probed his back with her fingers.

Fin-Kedinn hissed. His eyes were closed, his skin clammy and grey. He was breathing shallowly, and Torak could see that every breath, in and out, was a knife in his side.

'Will he live?' Torak said in a low voice.

Renn glared at him.

'Is he bleeding inside?' he whispered.

'I don't know. If he bleeds from his mouth . . . '

Fin-Kedinn's lips twisted in a wry smile. 'Then it's over. Saeunn was right. I won't reach the Deep Forest.'

'Don't talk,' warned Renn.

'Hurts less than breathing,' said her uncle. 'Where are we?'

Torak told him.

He groaned. 'Ah, not here! Not the hill!'

'We can't move you, not tonight,' said Renn.

'This is a bad place,' muttered Fin-Kedinn. 'Haunted. Evil.'

'No more talk!' admonished Renn, cutting strips from the hem of her jerkin for bandages.

Wolf lay beside her, his muzzle between his paws. Rip and Rek stalked up and down at a stiff raven walk. Torak watched Fin-Kedinn turning his head from side to side. He'd never felt so powerless.

Renn told him to fetch wood for a fire, and he ran off. His hands were shaking and he kept dropping sticks. He thought, if that beech had fallen just a little differently, it would have crushed his breastbone, and we'd be putting on Death Marks. It would be my fault. I could have killed us all.

From where he stood, the hill sloped down to the Blackwater. A deer trail wound along its bank, past one of the stone jaws and into the Deep Forest. He pictured the Oak Mage vanishing into the shadows. He had been so close.

Back at the ledge, Fin-Kedinn had slipped into an uneasy doze, and Renn was on her knees with a handful of birch-bark tinder, grimly trying and failing to get a spark with her strike-fire. 'Well, go on then,' she said without looking up.

'What do you mean?' said Torak.

'Go after him. That's what you want.'

He stared at her. 'I'm not leaving you.'

'But you want to.'

He flinched.

'It'll take days to get Fin-Kedinn back to the clan,' she said, still failing to get a spark. 'And all the time, Thiazzi's getting away. That's what you're thinking, isn't it?'

'Renn –'

'You never wanted us to come!' she burst out. 'Well, here's your chance to be rid of us!'

'Renn!'

They faced each other, white and shaking.

'I won't leave you,' said Torak. 'In the morning I'll bring round the canoes. Then we'll work out what to do.'

Savagely, Renn struck a spark. Her lips trembled as she blew life into it.

Torak went down on his knees and helped feed the fire with kindling, then sticks. When it was fully awake, he took her hand, and she gripped so hard that it hurt.

'He's beaten us,' she said.

'For now,' he replied.

Night deepened, and the sliver of moon fled across the sky. Renn said they should take comfort from it; it would grow stronger, and so would Fin-Kedinn. Torak thought she was trying very hard to persuade herself.

While she tended Fin-Kedinn, he fetched their gear from the canoes, then used branches to turn the ledge into a rough shelter, leaving a gap for the smoke. He'd found a clump of comfrey near the river, and Renn pounded its roots into a poultice, while Torak made the leaves into a strengthening brew in a swiftly fashioned birch-bark bowl. Together, they bandaged Fin-Kedinn's ribs. The binding had to be tight, to help set the broken bones. When it was done, all three of them were sweating and pale.

After that, Renn fed the fire with juniper boughs and wafted some of the smoke into the shelter to drive off the worms of sickness. Torak tucked a slip of dried horse meat in a crack in a boulder to thank the Forest for letting his foster father live. Then, as they were both famished, they shared more meat. Fin-Kedinn did not eat at all.

The moon set, and his restlessness increased. 'Don't let the fire die,' he murmured. 'Renn. Draw lines of power around the shelter.'

Renn gave Torak a worried look. If his wits were wandering, it was a bad sign.

Torak noticed that the ravens hadn't settled to roost, but were hopping warily among the rocks, while Wolf lay at the mouth of the shelter, watching the dark beyond the firelight. Torak had the uneasy sense that they were on guard.

Renn took her medicine pouch and went to draw the lines.

'Don't go far,' warned Fin-Kedinn.

Torak fed the fire another stick. 'You said this was a bad place. What did you mean?'

Fin-Kedinn watched the flames. 'Nothing grows here now. Nothing has since – the demons were forced back into the rocks.' He paused. 'But they're close, Torak. They want to get out.'

Torak dipped a clump of moss in the cup and cooled his foster father's brow. Renn would be angry if he let Fin-Kedinn talk, but he had to know. 'Tell me,' he said.

Fin-Kedinn coughed, and Torak held his shoulders. When it was over, the skin around the Raven Leader's eyes had a bluish tinge. 'Many summers ago,' he said, 'this hill was thick with trees. Birch, rowan, in cracks between the rocks. Holding the demons inside.' He shifted position and winced. 'Souls' Night. Long past. People came to let them out.'

Renn returned and knelt beside him. 'But the demons couldn't get out, could they?' she said. 'I feel them under the rocks, very close.'

'One man stopped them,' said Fin-Kedinn. 'He set a fire on the hill. Banished the demons back into the rocks. But the fire escaped.' He licked his lips. 'Terrible . . . It can leap into a tree faster than a lynx, and when it does — when it gets into the branches — it goes where it likes. You wouldn't believe how fast. It ate the whole valley.'

Torak began to be afraid. 'Was anyone hurt?'

Fin-Kedinn nodded. 'Trapped. Terrible burns. One killed.' He grimaced, as if he smelt charred flesh.

Torak peered into the dark. 'What *is* this place?' he whispered.

'Don't you know?' said Fin-Kedinn.

The hairs on Torak's arms prickled. 'Is this where . . . '

'Yes. This is where your father shattered the fire-opal. Where he broke the power of the Soul-Eaters.'

Out in the night, a vixen screamed. From far away came the deep oo-hu, oo-hu of an owl. Torak and Renn exchanged glances. It was an eagle owl.

Renn said, 'When I was drawing the lines of power, I felt a presence. Not only demons. Something else. Lost. Searching.'

'There are ghosts here,' said Fin-Kedinn. 'The one who died.'

Flames leapt in Renn's dark eyes. 'The seventh Soul-Eater.'

The Raven Leader made no reply.

An ember collapsed in a shower of sparks. Torak jumped. 'Were you here that night?' he said.

'No.' Pain contracted Fin-Kedinn's features. Torak didn't think it was caused by his broken ribs. 'After the great fire,' Fin-Kedinn went on, 'your mother and father sought me. They begged me to help them get away.'

Renn put her hand on his shoulder. 'You need to rest. Don't talk any more.'

'No! I must tell this!' He spoke with startling force, and his burning blue gaze held Torak's. 'I was angry. I wanted revenge against him for – for taking your mother. I turned them away.'

Torak heard the click of raven talons on stone. He looked into the face of his foster father and wanted it not to be true, and knew that it was.

'Next day,' said Fin-Kedinn, 'I relented. I went after them. But they'd gone. Fled to the Deep Forest.' He shut his eyes. 'I never saw them again. If I'd helped them, she might have lived.'

Torak touched his hand. 'You couldn't have known what would happen.'

The Raven Leader's smile was bitter. 'So you tell yourself. Does it help?'

Wolf leapt up with a growl and sped after a quarry only he could sense. An ember dislodged from the fire. Torak nudged it back with his boot. Suddenly, the light seemed a fragile shield against the dark.

'Keep the fire bright,' said Fin-Kedinn. 'And stay awake. Demons. Ghosts. They know we're here.'

The Chosen One watches the unbelievers sleep, and hungers to punish them and set the fire free.

The girl who woke the fire did it wrongly and without respect. She is an unbeliever. She does not follow the True Way.

The boy threw a branch at the fire and kicked it. He too has lost the Way.

The Master shall know of this. The Master honours the fire, and the fire honours him. The Master will punish the unbelievers.

The fire is sacred. It must be honoured, for it is the purity and the truth. The Chosen One loves the fire for its terrible glare and its hunger for the Forest, for its dreadful caress. The Chosen One longs to be one with the fire again.

The wind changes and the Chosen One moves to crouch in the breath of the fire, to drink its sacred bitterness. The Chosen One's hand cups ash. The ash is acrid on the tongue, heavy in the belly. It is the power and the truth.

The injured man moans in painful dreams. The boy's sleep is also troubled, but the girl slumbers as one dead. And over them, wolf and raven keep watch – while the fire sinks untended. Dishonoured.

Anger kindles in the breast of the Chosen One.

The unbelievers are evil.

They must be punished.

EIGHT

Torak woke before dawn. The fire had burned low. The others were still asleep. Renn lay on her side, one arm flung out. Fin-Kedinn was frowning, as if even sleeping hurt. Both looked disturbingly vulnerable.

Quietly, Torak wriggled out of his sleeping-sack and crawled from the shelter.

Below him on the slope, a wolverine rose on its hind legs to snuff his scent, then bounded off. This told Torak that Wolf must have gone hunting. If he'd been near, the wolverine would have stayed away. With a twinge of apprehension, Torak wondered what else might have managed to creep close.

Below him the valley of the Blackwater floated in mist. The Forest rang with birdsong, but the ravens were gone.

On the hill, he could see nothing except naked rock. He climbed to the crown. Nothing. Only an ancient tree stump on the western slope, its roots still clinging to the demon-haunted cracks. He thought of his father, who had sparked the events that had brought him to this place. He was shocked to realize that he could scarcely remember Fa's face.

As light crept into the sky, he spotted a faint dew trail of booted feet. Drawing his knife, he followed it round to the overhang above the shelter. Near the edge, he found a small cone of fine grey ash. He frowned. Someone had poured it with care, like an offering. Someone who had watched them in the night.

He caught a flicker of movement in the mist by the river. His heart contracted.

Someone stood on the bank, staring up at him. The face was indistinct; the hair long, pale. An arm rose. A finger pointed at him. Accusing.

Torak touched the medicine pouch at his hip and felt the shape of the horn within. Sheathing his knife, he started down the hill. He dreaded coming face to face with Bale's ghost. But maybe it would speak to him. Maybe he could say he was sorry.

The birds had stopped singing. On either side of the trail, hemlock floated in vaporous white.

Footsteps heading his way.

A wild-eyed man burst from the mist and blundered into him. 'Help me!' he gasped, clutching Torak's parka and glancing back over his shoulder.

Staggering under his weight, Torak breathed the stink of blood and terror.

'Help me!' pleaded the man. 'They – they – '

'Who?' said Torak.

'The Deep Forest!' Blood sprayed Torak's face as the man brandished his stump. *They cut off my hand!*

‡‡

'You'd be mad to go in there,' snarled the man as Renn finished binding his stump. He'd stopped shaking, but whenever an ember cracked, he cringed.

He said his name was Gaup of the Salmon Clan. His parka and leggings were muddy fish-skin lined with squirrel fur, and one cheek bore the sinuous tattoo of his clan. Around his neck he wore a band of sweat-blackened salmon-skin, and small fish bones were braided into his fair hair, reminding Torak of Bale.

'And it was Deep Forest people who did this?' said Fin-Kedinn. He sat with his back against a rock, haggard, breathing through clenched teeth.

'They swore that if they saw me again, it'd be my head.'

'But they made sure you survived,' said Renn. 'They seared the wound with hot stone so that you wouldn't bleed to death.'

'So I should thank them?' retorted Gaup.

'How about thanking Renn for sewing up your stump?' said Torak.

Gaup glared. He hadn't thanked Torak either, for helping him to the shelter and giving him food and water. And Torak hadn't missed the smear of ash on the heel of his boot.

Out loud, Torak said, 'When you were in the Deep Forest, did you see a man in a dugout? A big man, very strong.'

'What do I care about that?' snapped Gaup. 'I was looking for my child! Four summers old, and they took her!'

Torak glanced at Renn. She'd had the same thought. Soul-Eaters took children as hosts for demons. To make tokoroths.

Fin-Kedinn shifted position. Torak could see that his thoughts were racing. 'To cut off a hand,' he said, 'that's a punishment from the bad times after the Great Wave. The clans forbade it long ago. Who did this to you?'

'The Auroch Clan.'

'*What?*' The Raven Leader was incredulous.

'I thought they were going to help me,' said Gaup. 'They gave me food. Told me to rest by their fire. Then they said I was in league with the Forest Horses. Accused *me* of stealing one of *their* children.'

More stolen children, thought Torak. Thiazzi's flight to the Deep Forest seemed to be turning into something else.

'They said the Forest Horses started it,' Gaup went on. 'The Forest Horses planted a curse stick, and claimed the land between the Blackwater and the Windriver as their range. The Aurochs burnt the curse stick. Then the Forest Horse Mage died of a sickness, and the new Mage found a dart in the corpse. Now all the clans have taken sides. Everyone has to wear a headband: green for Auroch and Lynx, brown for Forest Horse and Bat.' He peered suspiciously at Torak's buckskin headband.

'When you were with the Aurochs,' said Torak, 'was there a big man among them?'

'Why do you keep asking?' said Gaup. Awkwardly, he crawled towards the doorway. 'I've wasted enough time, I'm going to fetch my clan. We'll *make* them give her back!'

'Gaup, wait,' commanded Fin-Kedinn. 'We'll go together. You and me.'

Renn and Torak stared at him. So did Gaup.

'We'll find your clan,' said the Raven Leader, 'and we'll

find mine. We'll get your daughter back — without shedding more blood.'

'How?' demanded Gaup. 'They won't listen, they're not *like* us!'

'Gaup,' Fin-Kedinn said firmly. 'This is what we will do.'

Gaup's shoulders sagged. Suddenly he was just an injured man who needed someone else to make the decisions.

After that, things happened fast. Torak fetched one of the canoes, and he and Renn helped Fin-Kedinn down to the river. Renn made him as comfortable as she could in the canoe, giving him willow bast to chew against fever, and hazelnuts to keep up his strength. Torak could see that she was sick with worry.

'How will you manage?' she asked her uncle when Gaup was out of earshot.

'We're heading downriver,' said Fin-Kedinn. 'The current will take us.'

'And if Gaup gets ill and is too weak to paddle?'

'He'll be all right,' Torak told her. 'You're a better healer than you think.'

'You only say that because you want this,' she retorted. 'Because it leaves you free to hunt Thiazzi.'

Torak did not reply. She was right.

Renn threw him a look and marched up to the canoe. 'I'm coming with you,' she told Fin-Kedinn.

'No,' he said. 'Torak needs you more.'

Torak was astonished. 'You'd let her come with me? After I nearly got you killed when I didn't see that trap?'

'You made a mistake,' said Fin-Kedinn. 'Don't make another.'

'But you can barely walk!' cried Renn. 'What if something happens? What if . . . ' She couldn't bring herself to go on.

'Renn,' said Fin-Kedinn. 'Can't you see that there's more at stake now than me or you or Torak? Thiazzi isn't merely hiding in the Deep Forest, he's up to something. It's Torak's destiny to stop him. He'll need your help.'

He spoke in the tone that brooked no refusal, and Renn didn't argue. But soon afterwards she ran off, unable to watch him leave.

'What will you do?' Torak asked his foster father when she'd gone.

'Try to stop a war,' said Fin-Kedinn.

War. Torak hardly knew what it meant. 'You think it's as bad as that?'

'Don't you? The Deep Forest clans no longer trust the Open, not after the sickness and the demon bear. If the Salmon Clan moves against them, it could be the spark that lights the tinder.' A spasm of pain took hold, and he gripped the side of the canoe. 'Listen to me, Torak. Find the Red Deer Clan. For your mother's sake, they'll help you. If you can't find them, find the Auroch Mage. His clan acted savagely, but I'm certain he didn't sanction it. I know him. He's a good man.'

Gaup returned, impatient to be off, and Torak helped him into the canoe.

'Find your mother's clan,' repeated Fin-Kedinn. 'Till you do, stay hidden. Climb trees if you have to; Deep Forest people are like deer, they seldom look up. And do *not* harm any of the black forest horses. The black ones are sacred. It's forbidden even to touch them.' Then he did something he'd never done before. He grasped Torak's hand.

Torak couldn't speak. Fa had done the same thing as he lay dying.

'Torak . . .' The blue eyes pierced his. 'You seek

vengeance. But don't let it take over your spirit.'

With his paddle, Gaup pushed the canoe away from the bank, forcing Torak to let go of his foster father's hand.

'Vengeance burns, Torak,' said Fin-Kedinn as the river bore him away. 'It burns your heart. It makes the pain worse. Don't let that happen to you.'

Renn had run up the slope towards the shelter. She couldn't bear to watch the Blackwater take her uncle away.

Then she'd changed her mind and raced down again. She was too late. Fin-Kedinn had gone.

In a daze, she went back to the shelter. She shouldered her sleeping-sack, quiver and bow, and stamped out the fire. She told herself that Gaup would get Fin-Kedinn safely back to the clan. But the truth was anything could happen. Fin-Kedinn might succumb to a fever, or start bleeding inside. Gaup might abandon him. She might never see him again.

When she reached the river, Torak was gone, probably to fetch the other canoe. She couldn't face doing nothing, so she dumped her sleeping-sack and stumbled along the trail that led to the Deep Forest.

She stopped well short of the gaping jaws. The mist had lifted, and the rocks glittered in the sun. To her left, a slope of alders and birch whispered secrets. To her right, the Blackwater snaked slyly past. Twenty paces ahead, the spruce trees of the Deep Forest warded her back. They were taller than their Open Forest sisters, and beneath their mossy arms, shadows shifted ceaselessly.

Torak had once reached the borders of the Deep Forest, but Renn had never been this close. It filled her with dread.

58

The Deep Forest was different. Its trees were more awake, its clans more suspicious; it was said to shelter creatures which had long since vanished elsewhere. And in summer, the World Spirit stalked its valleys as a tall man with the antlers of a stag.

Out of nowhere, Rip and Rek swooped, startling her. Then they were off, disappearing into the sky with caws of alarm.

Renn couldn't see anything wrong, but just in case, she moved off the trail, behind a juniper bush.

At the edge of the Deep Forest, the shadows beneath the spruce trees coalesced – and became a man. Then another. And another.

Renn held her breath.

The hunters emerged without making a sound. Their wovenbark clothes were mottled brown and green, like leaves on the Forest floor; Renn found it hard to tell where men ended and trees began. Each hunter wore a green headband – she couldn't remember whose side that was – and each head was obscured by a fine green net. These hunters had no faces. They were not human.

One raised his hand, his green-stained fingers flickering in a complex signal that meant nothing to Renn. The others headed up the slope to her left.

A hunter passed within a few paces of where she crouched. She saw his thin slate axe and his long green bow. She smelt tallow and wood-ash, and caught the glint of eyes behind the net. She saw how it sucked in and out where the mouth should be.

From the Deep Forest, another faceless hunter emerged, this one carrying a spear. When he was five paces from Renn, he thrust it into the ground with such force that it quivered.

At head height, the spear-shaft bore a bundle of leaves which Renn recognized as poisonous nightshade. From this dangled something dark, the size of a fist.

The hunter shook the spear to make sure that it was firmly planted, and walked back into the Deep Forest.

Renn's gorge rose.

The thing hanging from the spear *was* a fist. It was Gaup's severed hand.

The meaning of the curse stick was clear. *The way is shut.*

Renn couldn't take her eyes off the hand. She thought about living the rest of her life like Gaup. Unable ever to use her bow again . . .

A movement to her right.

Her heart lurched.

Torak was walking up the trail towards her.

NINE

Sweat slid down Renn's sides.

Torak was walking up the trail, looking for her. He hadn't seen the hunters on the slope, the trees blocked his view, and for the same reason, the hunters hadn't seen him. But they would, in about fifteen paces, when he reached that patch of sunlight where a fallen birch had left a gap.

Quiet as cloudshadow, the hunters spread across the slope, melting into wind-tossed shade and sun-dappled leaves. Renn dared not shout or make the redstart warning call. She couldn't throw a stone at Torak without standing up.

Suddenly, he stopped. He'd seen the curse stick.

Swiftly, he stepped off the trail, and kept moving, getting closer to the gap.

Renn had no choice. She had to warn him, despite the

risk. She whistled the redstart call.

Torak vanished in the bushes.

She felt rather than saw the hunters turn towards her. Like well-aimed spears, their gaze converged on her hiding-place. How had they known it wasn't a real bird? She'd added the uplift at the end which she and Torak used to distinguish it, but no-one else had ever noticed that. They must be unbelievably observant. And suspicious.

The hunters started down the slope towards her.

Her mind darted in panic. Her body ached to run, but she knew that her only hope was not to move. Keep still, wait till they were almost upon her – *then* run like a hare, jump in the river – and pray to the guardian.

They were spreading out to surround her. She tensed to run.

Another redstart whistle, behind them on the slope.

The blank heads turned.

There it was again. It had to be Torak. Renn recognized the uplift at the end. Somehow, he'd found his way behind them.

Holding her breath, she watched them climb towards the sound.

Again the call came, but this time it was in the reeds by the river. How could that be? Torak couldn't have moved that fast.

Suddenly a shadow swept over her, and Rek alighted in an alder near the curse stick, whistling like a redstart.

The hunters paused. Painted fingers flickered in silent speech. They started down, heading for the tree where the raven perched. They passed within three paces of Renn's juniper without sensing her presence. Their ferocious intent blasted her like heat.

Rek gave another perfect imitation of the redstart

signal, and as they drew near, she flew off with a harsh raven laugh.

Silently, the faceless hunters watched her go. Then they headed up the trail and vanished into the Deep Forest.

'Are you all right?' said Torak, grasping her shoulder.

Renn nodded. She was shaking, clenching her teeth to stop them chattering.

'Let's get out of here,' muttered Torak.

They retreated to an alder thicket. 'They'll have found our tracks,' said Renn when she could trust herself to speak. 'They'll know we're here.'

Torak shook his head. 'They'll think we went with Fin-Kedinn.' He told her how he'd left the remaining canoe downstream, judging it too conspicuous to take into the Deep Forest, and had hidden their gear and covered their tracks.

'How did you know they'd come?' said Renn.

'I didn't. Didn't even know they were there till I heard you call. But I got used to covering my tracks when I was outcast. Come on. I'm hungry. Last chance for hot food.'

It hadn't occurred to Renn that once they were in the Deep Forest, they'd have to do without fire. Feeling childish and ignorant, she went off to forage. They ought to save their supplies for the days ahead; at least she'd thought of that.

When she got back, Torak had woken up a fire. He'd set it under a rock facing away from the Deep Forest, and used only small, dry pieces of beech, without the bark, so that it burned almost without smoke.

Renn thought, he learned these things when he was

outcast. It made her feel as if she didn't really know him.

Food steadied her a bit. She made a stew of chickweed, bittercress and bramble shoots, with meaty spring mushrooms, and woodpigeon eggs and snails baked in the embers. The snails were particularly delicious, as they'd been feeding on crow garlic.

While they ate, Rip and Rek took their morning bath in the shallows, flicking water over themselves with their wings, and splashing Wolf, who'd returned from hunting and lay on the bank, pretending not to notice.

Renn gave Rek a peeled egg and whispered her thanks. Then to Torak, 'Who *were* those people?'

'Aurochs, I think. Green headbands, and one had a horn amulet.' He asked her about the spear in the trail, and she told him it was a curse stick. 'If you pass it without the proper charm, you fall sick and die. You can't *see* the curse, but it's there. It draws fever demons like moths to a flame.'

He thought about that. 'Can you get us past?'

The knot in her belly tightened. 'Maybe.' In fact, she doubted it. The Deep Forest had the best mages of all. She would be no match for them. 'But they won't rely on curse sticks,' she added. 'They'll keep watch.'

He didn't reply. Often, when he was working up to say something, he would run his thumb over the scar on his forearm. He was doing it now. 'Renn . . . '

'*Don't* say it,' she broke in.

'What?'

'He wasn't my kin, I don't have to go with you, it's too dangerous, I might get killed.'

He set his jaw. 'It *is* too dangerous. And it's not just them, it's me. Look what happened to Fin-Kedinn. Next time it could be you.'

She began to protest, but he talked over her. 'There's

something else. We were watched in the night. I found a trail and a pile of ash.'

'*Ash?*' She tried to conceal her alarm. 'Do you think it was Gaup?'

'I did at first. Now I'm not sure.'

She realized what he was doing. 'You're trying to put me off. Why must you always do this? Do you think it'll work? Do you think I'll say, Oh, well, in that case I'm going back to my clan?'

'That's what you should do. Yes.'

'Well I won't!'

He glared at her. In the morning light his face looked older. Ruthless. 'Renn. I warn you. I'll do whatever it takes to get Thiazzi.'

'Fine,' she retorted. 'Let's get started. We'll need a disguise. We're on the Aurochs' side of the river, so we'd better try to look like them.'

He gave a curt nod. 'Right,' he said.

羊丰

'There,' said Renn. 'I defy even an Auroch to spot you now.' She was being very practical and brisk, but Torak wasn't fooled. She was as scared as he was.

Over the winter, Fin-Kedinn had taught them a few tricks about concealment. It had taken all afternoon to put them into practice. Renn turned out to be extremely good at it, which Torak found unnerving. She seemed to have a Mage's skill for making things appear other than what they were.

First, she'd made a greenish-brown stain of lichen and river clay, taking the clay from below the waterline, so that no-one would notice. She'd mixed it with wood-ash and the marrowfat salve, to mask their scent and make it waterproof. Then she'd unpicked her clan-creature feathers and tucked them inside her jerkin, and they'd daubed the stain on each other's faces, throats, hands and clothes, dappling it in blotches: some light, some darkened with charcoal.

They knew from clan meets that Aurochs daubed their scalps with yellow clay to resemble bark, so they tucked their hair inside their parkas and did the same. They didn't have time to make nets for their faces, so they simply stained Torak's headband green and made one for Renn. Next, they padded their quivers with moss to prevent the arrows rattling, and agreed a new warning signal. Finally, Torak cut them hogweed breathing tubes, in case they had to hide underwater.

When it was done, Wolf approached Torak cautiously, gave a tentative sniff, and jerked back in alarm.

It's me, Torak told him in wolf talk.

Wolf flattened his ears and growled.

It's me. Come here.

Warily, Wolf moved closer.

Torak breathed softly on his muzzle, talking in wolf talk and person talk. It took a while before Wolf was reassured.

'He didn't know you,' Renn said in a strained voice.

Torak tried to smile, but his face felt stiff beneath its disguise. 'Do I look so different?'

'You look frightening.'

He met her eyes. 'So do you.' Her smooth green face was disturbingly like her mother's. She even moved differently. Her body, her hands, seemed fraught with mysterious power. He thought that if he touched her, he might burn his fingers.

'Do you think it'll work?' she said.

He cleared his throat. 'At a distance, maybe. Not up

66

close. The best defence will be –'

'Not getting caught.' She flashed him her sharp-toothed grin, and was Renn again.

Dusk fell, and the half-eaten moon rose above the trees. Moths flitted among glowing white campions. High in a spruce tree, Torak heard the hungry cheeping of woodpecker nestlings.

'Now for the charm,' said Renn.

In the faint moonlight, Gaup's severed hand turned slowly on its cord. It should have been crawling with ants and flies, but there were none. Such was the power of the curse that no creature would touch it.

Torak stood watch with Wolf, while Renn approached the curse stick, keeping to the shadows and placing her feet on dock leaves to obscure her prints. She clutched a bundle of wormwood and rowan twigs, and as she squatted near the stick, she muttered the charm and struck the spear-shaft over and over with the bundle.

The river flowed more quietly. The trees stilled to listen. Torak felt the curse hanging heavy in the air. He worried that Renn was too close; that it might be seeping into her skin.

She broke off with a gasp. 'I can't,' she whispered.

'Yes you can!' he urged.

'I'm not strong enough.'

He waited.

She went on. At last, she heaved a ragged sigh, rose, and threw the bundle in the river.

'Did it work?' said Torak.

'I don't know. We'll soon find out.'

They withdrew, taking care to brush away their tracks. It seemed to Torak that a tension had leached from the darkness.

Wolf padded towards the curse stick and sat gazing up at the bloody hand. Without warning, he seized it in his jaws, worried it to make sure it was dead, and trotted off to eat in peace. Soon afterwards, they heard a flurry in the undergrowth and an irritable growl; then Rip and Rek flew off, each bearing a finger in their beaks.

Torak unclenched his fists. 'I think it worked.'

'Maybe,' said Renn.

They went to fetch their gear.

'We'll go in after moonset,' said Torak.

Renn didn't reply, but he knew what she was thinking. They still had no plan for getting past any watching Aurochs.

Above him in the spruce tree, the woodpecker nestlings called tirelessly for food. Torak saw that their parents had been clever, pecking the hole under a bracket mushroom which made a roof to keep off the rain, and choosing a hollow tree riddled with more holes, so they'd have lots of escape routes if a marten attacked. He remembered Fin-Kedinn's lessons on concealment. *The first rule is to learn from other creatures.*

The male woodpecker flew in with nightmeal for his children, spotted Torak, and sped to another tree some distance away, where he perched, calling loudly, kik-kik-kik! *Not that tree, this one!*

'I think,' said Torak, 'I've got an idea.'

The moon had set, the wind had dropped. The trees stood breathless. Waiting.

Torak knelt beside Wolf and told him in wolf talk that they needed to hide from everyone, but were still hunting the Bitten One. He wasn't sure if he got it across.

Rising to his feet, he nodded at Renn. She nodded back.

Keeping off the trail, they started upriver. They passed the curse stick. They drew level with the great stone jaws.

A squirrel scampered up a tree. A roe buck fled, flashing its white rump.

Good, thought Torak. Maybe the Aurochs aren't so close.

Maybe.

Renn walked beside him, silent as a shadow. Wolf's paws made no sound.

The spruce trees waited for them, their arms dripping with dark clots of moss.

Torak paused. He thought of the Oak Mage. He thought of Bale. He took a breath and entered the Deep Forest.

TEN

Wolf's hackles rose. Torak glanced at Renn to make sure that she'd seen. She had.

Bitten One, said Wolf.

Near? said Torak.

Many lopes.

Torak bent close to Renn. 'He's picked up Thiazzi's trail,' he whispered, 'but he's far away.'

'And still no Aurochs?'

He shook his head.

She was puzzled. So was he. They'd been creeping between the shadowy trees for ever, following the river upstream, but staying well back from its banks. So far, no sign of Aurochs. The trees, though . . . Roots snagged Torak's boots. Twig fingers brushed his face. It was warmer in the Deep Forest. The air smelt greener, more alive. Bats flitted overhead, and the undergrowth stirred with secret rustlings. Moss dripped from every branch and log and boulder – as if, thought Torak, a great green tide had drowned the Forest and then receded. And behind it all, he felt the immense, watching presence of the trees.

Wolf turned aside and ran to an ash tree. Rising on his hind legs, he put both forepaws on the trunk and sniffed a low-hanging branch. *Odd*, he told Torak with a twitch of his whiskers.

Torak touched the branch. His fingers came away slimy, smelling strangely of earth.

Renn pointed to the branch. *What is it?*

He shook his head, wiping his hand on his leggings and wishing he hadn't touched it. Deep Forest clans were known for their skill with poisons.

They reached a grove of murmuring alders. As they entered, the trees fell silent, as if they didn't want to be overheard.

Wolf halted and snuffed the air.

Bitten One. Over the Wet.

Torak was still taking that in when Wolf lowered his head.

Den.

Beyond the alders, Torak glimpsed shadows moving in blackness. Bulky shapes that might be shelters.

'Camp!' Renn breathed in his ear.

'And Wolf says Thiazzi is *across* the river, in Forest Horse territory.'

'We have to go back,' she urged, 'cross downstream.'

That risked confusing Wolf and losing Thiazzi's trail, but they had no choice. They started to backtrack.

At least, they tried, but Torak got the sense that they'd lost their way. The gurgle of the river seemed fainter, and he caught the sharp, unmistakeable scent of crow garlic, which they hadn't encountered on the way in.

He strained to pierce the gloom. A dock leaf skewered on a twig glimmered in starlight. A whisper of air cooled his cheek as an owl or a bat swept past.

That leaf.

He stopped so abruptly that Renn walked into him.

'What is it?'

'Not sure. *Don't* move.'

That twig could not have speared the leaf by chance. It pierced the leaf blade like a needle, straight down its length, to the right of the midrib. It had to be a signal.

To the right of the midrib.

He glanced to his right, saw only a dim lattice of branches.

There.

Ahead, to the right, a sapling had been bent back and secured by a deft arrangement of crossed sticks. Mounted at its tip was a vicious spike. From the crossed sticks, near-invisible, a rope stretched across his path at chest height. Another step and he would have sprung the trap, releasing the sapling and sending the spike plunging into his side.

Torak licked his lips. They tasted chalky from the disguise. He showed Renn the trap. Her hand went to her shoulder, where her clan-creature feathers had been.

They had to push through junipers to get around the trap, which had been cunningly set between the thorny bushes, to drive its victim towards it. When they were through, Renn hissed, 'This isn't the way we came.'

'I know. And it was sheer luck I spotted that trap.' He didn't need to say it: how many more lay in wait?

Wolf turned his head towards the river, and they followed his gaze. Did that shadow just move?

A moment later, starlight glinted on a spearhead.

The Auroch hunter was maybe twenty paces away, walking upstream. Torak and Renn sank into the bracken – slowly, so as not to attract attention by sudden movement. Torak's mind raced. Upriver lay the Auroch camp. Downriver, the way back to the Open Forest, and maybe more lethal traps. On the riverbank, at least one Auroch hunter was keeping watch.

Renn voiced his thoughts. 'We'll have to try your plan right here.'

'Could you make the shots?'

'I think so. If we climb a tree.'

He nodded.

Renn found a tall lime that looked easier to climb than the others, as it had an odd snake of thickened bark rippling down its trunk. 'Lightning-struck,' she murmured, 'but it survived. Maybe that'll bring us luck.'

We'll need it, thought Torak. His plan was simple, and if it worked, their decoys would draw the Aurochs north, away from the Blackwater, allowing them to slip across.

If it worked. He was losing faith fast.

Linking his hands, he boosted Renn into the tree. Then he knelt and told Wolf to stay close, to come back in the Light – and be alert for traps.

Wolf's breath warmed his face as his muzzle brushed his eyelids. *Stay safe, pack-brother*, he told Torak.

He was so trusting. And Torak was leading him into terrible danger.

On impulse, Torak took his medicine horn from its pouch, shook out a little earthblood, and daubed it on Wolf's forehead, where he couldn't lick if off. *Stay safe, pack-brother*, he said. Putting his hand on the lime's rough bark, he begged the Forest to protect Wolf.

The lightning scar was thicker than his wrist, and he climbed it like a rope. He felt the tree sensing their presence. He asked it not to give them away. Below him, Wolf's silver eyes glowed. Then he vanished into the dark.

Huddled in a fork made by three great limbs, Torak and Renn kept their sleeping-sacks rolled, relying on their reindeer-hide clothes to stay warm. 'We'll wait here till morning,' whispered Torak, 'less chance of being seen.' And less chance of escape if they *were* seen, but neither of them mentioned that.

Renn pointed to a tall spruce north of the Aurochs' camp. Its upper branches spiked the stars; they should catch the rising sun. From her quiver she drew one of the arrows she'd prepared.

As she took aim, her face tensed with concentration. Her disguise made her alien: as if, thought Torak, she'd become Deep Forest.

Her bow creaked. She lowered it again. The night was too quiet. The Aurochs might hear the twang.

At last a gust of wind woke the trees. She took aim and let fly. The arrow struck the spruce and its burden swung free on the cord tied to the shaft. Renn nocked another arrow and hit another tree, further east; then another and another, each time waiting for the breeze to cover the sound.

Now they had to wait till dawn, and hope the plan worked.

They didn't have another.

In the darkness, firelight flared.

Renn gripped Torak's arm. The Auroch camp was much

closer than they'd thought.

High in the lime tree, they watched tall figures moving with the silent purposefulness of ants. Several gathered round a tree in the centre of camp, smearing something dark on its lower branches. Two more knelt to waken another fire.

Torak was mystified. Why waken one from scratch when you could take a burning branch from the first? And they weren't using strike-fires. One man spun a stick between his palms, drilling it into a piece of wood on the ground which he held down with one foot, while he kept the drill straight by means of a cross-bar clamped between his teeth. It worked. Smoke curled. The second man fed the flames beard-moss, then kindling. When the fire was fully awake, everyone knelt and touched their foreheads to the ground.

More Aurochs emerged from the Forest. Torak counted five, seven, ten. Each man – and they were all men – bore an axe, a bow, two knives, and a shield: a narrow, arm-length wedge of wood, whose pointed end he thrust into the earth, before drawing off his netting hood to reveal a caked head and bizarrely ridged and furrowed face.

Torak broke out in a cold sweat. Gaup was right. These people were different.

And yet they were setting spits over the fires, and soon he smelt the delicious, familiar smell of roasting woodgrouse, weirdly at odds with the silent camp.

'Why don't they speak?' he whispered.

'I think it's to make them more tree-like,' breathed Renn. 'That's what Deep Forest people want above all: to be like the trees.'

'I can see more shields down there than men.'

She nodded and held up three fingers. Three hunters

still out there, stalking the Forest. They'd been right to climb the lime.

They took turns to stay awake. A thin rain pattered into Torak's dreams, and the Forest became a dark, soughing sea where night birds flitted like fishes. From far away came the oo-hu, oo-hu of an eagle owl.

Renn was shaking his shoulder. 'Dawn soon.'

He blinked, kneading cramp from his calf. The day was blustery, with a dry south wind. Chaffinches and warblers were already in full voice, the woodpigeons just beginning.

'I hope Rip and Rek are still asleep,' muttered Renn. 'The last thing we need is a raven greeting.'

Torak tried to smile. He thought it less and less likely that their plan would work. Even if it did, they'd have only a brief chance to swim the Blackwater, and then they'd be in Forest Horse territory. And all the time, Thiazzi was getting away.

Grey light seeped into camp, and Torak made out humped shelters around the central beech.

He peered at it. It couldn't be. Those lower branches were *red*. It wasn't the morning sun, the branches themselves – bark, twigs, leaves – had been daubed all over with earthblood. Why, he thought, would anyone paint an entire branch red?

No time to wonder. The sun was rising. Soon they must be on the move.

To the north, something glittered in the tall spruce tree. And there, further east. Renn flashed him an edgy grin. So far, the plan was working. The flint flakes they'd tied to her arrowshafts shimmered and clinked in the wind.

The Aurochs had seen them. Men were pointing, running for weapons and shields.

Swiftly, Torak and Renn climbed down to earth. Wolf appeared, his fur wet with dew. They headed for the river.

Willows overhung the Blackwater, holding in the night. There was no sign of Aurochs. Torak prayed that they'd all been drawn by the decoys. Yanking off their boots and tying them to their sleeping-sack rolls, they made their way down the bank and into the reeds, moving cautiously, so as not to startle any water birds into betraying them. The shallows were choked with leafy saplings felled by a flood further upstream.

'Good cover,' murmured Renn.

They risked strained smiles. Maybe this was going to work.

Bracing themselves for the cold, they waded into the river. Torak's feet sank into a freezing slime of dead leaves, and he saw Renn's stained lips tighten in disgust. He grabbed a floating sapling for cover. She did the same. They swam after Wolf, who was already halfway across.

The Blackwater wasn't as sleepy as it looked. It was a struggle to resist its stealthy underwater pull.

Suddenly Wolf veered, and came swimming *towards* them, his ears pinned back in alarm.

'What's *that*?' whispered Renn.

Torak's belly turned over. Those logs in midstream: they were floating *upriver*. And some of them had eyes.

One raised its head. Torak saw a fierce green face tattooed with leaves. A brown headband. Long hair braided with horse tails.

A Forest Horse raiding party. Heading straight for them.

ELEVEN

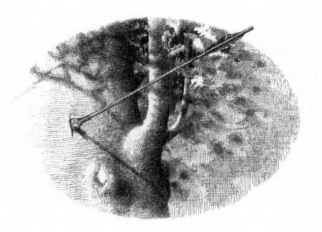

'Get underwater, head back to the bank,' Torak told Renn just before he dived. He couldn't find the breathing tube in his belt. Too bad, he'd hold his breath. He only hoped Renn had heard him.

She had. She surfaced soon after he did in the same patch of reeds, and they waited, gritting their teeth to stop them chattering.

The Forest Horses hadn't seen them. The green men lay on their bellies, paddling silently with their hands, knives clamped between charcoal-blackened teeth.

Not far from Torak, Wolf hauled himself onto the bank and shook himself noisily.

Eyes flicked sideways in leaf-tattooed faces, then back again. A lone wolf was no concern of theirs.

The reeds gave good cover, allowing Torak and Renn to

crawl up the bank and get their bearings. Torak was shocked. The treacherous Blackwater had carried them *nearer* the camp, not further away.

Soaked and shivering, he wondered what to do. Any moment now, the Aurochs would realize they'd been tricked and head back to the river, spreading out to hunt the unknown intruders. He and Renn would be trapped between them and the Forest Horses.

Unless he could steer both sides away from them.

'Head downriver,' he told Renn in a whisper. 'Wait for me past that bend, I'll meet you there.'

Her eyes widened. 'Where are you going?'

'No time to explain! Watch out for traps!'

Telling Wolf to stay with the pack-sister, he started towards the Auroch camp. When he was as close as he dared, he crouched and whipped two arrows from his quiver. Then he took out his medicine horn and quickly smeared the arrowshafts with earthblood. He had no idea what those red branches meant to the Aurochs, but they were easy to spot, which was all that mattered.

Still crouching, he nocked the first arrow to his bow and waited.

He glimpsed a Forest Horse hunter coming ashore: stealthily, keeping upright so that the water ran noiselessly down his body rather than pattering on leaves.

Torak took aim. He wasn't as good a shot as Renn, but he didn't need to be. His arrow thudded into a holly a good distance away.

The tattooed head turned to follow it.

From the corner of his eye, Torak saw an Auroch hunter making for the river. His belly tightened. They were faster than he'd thought. He loosed his second red arrow and hit another tree.

Without waiting to see the response, he fled, running fast and low to where Renn was waiting. If his trick worked, both sides would make for those mysterious red arrows, and then . . .

Shouts behind him, a clash of spears. He felt a spurt of savage joy. The Aurochs were fighting the Forest Horses, leaving him and Renn to cross the river and hunt Thiazzi.

Renn's shadowy figure beckoned from a dense stand of spruce, and he grabbed her hand. Her grasp was hot as ash as she led him through the gloom to the hiding-place she'd found: the hollow ruin of an enormous oak.

Panting, he collapsed against the tree, and as her fingers slipped from his, he gave a shaky laugh. 'That was *too* close!'

No reply. He was alone in the tree.

Twenty paces away, Wolf emerged from a clump of willows, followed by Renn, dripping wet and furious. 'Where,' she whispered, 'in the name of the Spirit have you *been?*'

TWELVE

'Who *was* that?' hissed Torak.

'Who was who?' demanded Renn. His disappearence had shaken her badly, and she was struggling not to show it.

'Someone took my hand. I thought it was you.'

'Well it wasn't.'

He grabbed her hand. 'Yours is cold, the other was hot.'

'Of course I'm cold, I'm soaking wet! Where did you *go?*'

From the Auroch camp came shouts, a scream of pain.

'Tell you later,' said Torak. 'Let's get across while we can.'

Renn was so cold that the Blackwater felt almost warm. The sodden gear on her back weighed her down, and the river was strong. As she reached the midstream, it sucked her under. She kicked to the surface, spluttering and spitting out leaves. Torak and Wolf were ahead and didn't notice.

The south bank was a forbidding tangle of willows, and as she neared it, her spirit quailed. She pictured leaf-faced hunters taking aim. She thought, Out of the cooking-skin and into the fire.

If the others were frightened, they gave no sign. Wolf scrambled up the bank, shook vigorously, and started casting for Thiazzi's scent. Torak waded noiselessly towards the willows.

Watching him scan the trees, Renn shivered. His disguise made him a creature of the Deep Forest: a dark-faced stranger with cold silver eyes.

He flicked her a glance and nodded – *clear* – then vanished into the willows. As she struggled to free her leg from a tangle of waterweed, he reached out and pulled her in.

'There's no-one here,' he said. 'I think they've all crossed to attack the camp.'

Hastily they dried themselves with grass, stuffing more down their boots and inside their clothes, to warm up. Torak cut some horsetail and scrubbed the green stain off their headbands, while Renn tended her poor, soaked bow.

Wolf found the scent and started south, away from the river and into a boggy woodland of alders rising from brown pools. Renn thought of traps and curse sticks and invisible hunters, and said a prayer to the guardian.

It was difficult country. They had to jump from one clump of alders to the next, and edge along fallen tree-trunks squelchy with moss. The water was clogged with frogspawn. Renn fell in and came out beslimed.

She tried to convince herself that this was a forest just like the one where she'd grown up. She saw a spruce tree whose fissured trunk was studded with cones jammed in by woodpeckers, so they could peck at the seeds. Open Forest woodpeckers did that, too. She spotted a pile of leaves near a badger's sett; the badgers had been cleaning up after the winter, and had dragged out their old bedding. All familiar, she told herself.

It didn't work. The trees murmured that she didn't belong. The woodpeckers were black.

Torak had found something.

Beneath an ash tree, the earth had been scraped to make a muddy wallow. It was five paces across, far bigger than even an auroch would make. Wolf snuffed it eagerly. Torak pushed his muzzle aside to examine a huge, round hoofprint. 'Some kind of giant auroch?' he said.

Renn nodded. 'Fin-Kedinn says there are creatures here that survived the Great Cold. I think they're called bison.'

He frowned. 'So they're prey?'

'I think so. But sometimes they charge.'

In the distance, an owl hooted. Oo-hu, oo-hu.

Renn caught her breath. In her mind, she saw the dread wooden face of the Eagle Owl Mage.

Torak was thinking the same thing. 'Could they be working together?' he said in a low voice. 'Thiazzi *and* Eostra?'

Renn hesitated. 'I'm not so sure. He's selfish. He'll want the fire-opal for himself. Besides, Saeunn told me – she can't be certain, but she thinks Eostra is in the Mountains.'

'And yet her owl is in the Deep Forest,' said Torak.

Renn was silent. She watched him rise to his feet and look about. She could see from his expression that whether Eostra was here or not, he was undeterred. He would find Thiazzi.

'Torak,' she said. 'What happened at the Auroch camp?

What did you do?'

Briefly, he told her how he'd set the two clans against each other. It was clever, but his ruthlessness shocked her. 'But – people might have been killed,' she said.

'That might have happened anyway.'

'Maybe. Or maybe the Forest Horses were only scouting, you don't know.'

'I warned you. I said I'd do whatever it takes to get Thiazzi.'

'Starting fights? Getting people killed?'

Wolf glanced doubtfully from one to the other.

Torak ignored him. 'Last spring,' he said, 'everyone was hunting me. This time, *I'm* doing the hunting. I swore an oath, Renn. So yes. I am ruthless. And if you can't take that, don't come with me!'

They went on in silence. Renn resolved not to be the first to speak.

The ground climbed steadily, and black spruce gave way to beech. They waded through waist-high nettles and clambered over rotting tree-trunks blistered with poisonous mushrooms. Renn noticed that the trees were taller than in the Open Forest, which would make them harder to climb; and the wood-ants didn't build their nests only on the south side of the trunks, but all around, which would make it easier to get lost.

No sign of people.

And yet . . .

Behind her a branch swayed, as if someone had edged out of sight.

She put her hand to her knife-hilt.

The branch stilled. If it was Forest Horse hunters, she thought, we'd know it by now.

Torak had gone ahead, and was kneeling to talk to Wolf. She ran to catch up. 'I saw something!' she panted.

'And Wolf smelt something,' said Torak. 'He says it smells like the Bright Beast.'

'That means fire.'

'It also means ash. The one who took my hand . . . it felt hot.'

Their eyes met.

'Whatever grabbed my hand,' said Torak. 'It's followed us across the river.'

As the light began to fail, they decided to pitch camp under a yew tree.

They'd reached a valley where beavers had dammed a stream to make a narrow lake. Renn saw the beavers' lodge in the middle: a sturdy pile of branches, some streaked yellow where they'd gnawed off the bark. She guessed it was still occupied, as a few willows remained along the shore. Fin-Kedinn said that beavers liked to eat all the willows before moving on.

Thinking of Fin-Kedinn hurt. She tried to imagine him safely back with the Ravens, busy with the salmon run, but her mind showed him grey-faced, hunched in the canoe. Maybe the worms of sickness were already eating into his marrow. And no Renn to chase them away.

Torak went scouting with Wolf, so to take her mind off Fin-Kedinn, she left her gear under the yew and went to forage. At least the plants were familiar. She gathered handfuls of succulent saxifrage and sharp-tasting sorrel;

and as they couldn't have a fire, she dug up spear thistle and silverweed roots, which they could eat raw.

Rip and Rek flew down, fluttering their wings and making famished gurgles, so she tossed them a couple of roots. Over the winter, she'd persuaded them to come when she called, but they would not yet perch on her shoulders, as they did with Torak.

Feeling slightly better, she went to refill the waterskins. The lake was sheened a dusty yellow with pollen, and around it, the trees leaned over to peer at their name-souls in the water. Renn held the skins down deep, to avoid scooping them up. It had never bothered her before, but here . . .

While the skins filled, she watched the ripples smoothing out, and wished Torak would come back and be Torak again: play tug-the-hide with Wolf, tease her about the freckle at the corner of her mouth. For the first time it struck her that his mother's father had been Oak Clan — which meant he was kin with Thiazzi. She wished she hadn't thought of that.

The waterskins were full. As she pulled them out, her name-soul stared back at her: an inscrutable, clay-headed Auroch.

A figure appeared behind it.

In one nightmare heartbeat, Renn took in clenched fists and a shock of long, pale hair.

With a cry she spun round.

Nothing. Just a stirring of willows, very close.

She whipped out her knife.

A branch creaked. Claws clattered on bark. She thought of tokoroths scurrying down trees, agile as spiders. She left the waterskins and raced back to camp.

Torak hadn't returned, but the ravens perched high in

the yew, cawing in distress. Her gear had been savagely attacked. Her quiver was slashed, its moss padding flung about, and most of her arrows had been snapped. Luckily, she'd hung her bow on the yew, and the attacker had missed it, but her sleeping-sack had been trampled into the dust, her tinder pouch cut to pieces, and her strike-fire smashed under a rock. Malice and rage throbbed in the air like sickness. And over everything lay a scattering of fine grey ash.

Drawing her axe, Renn backed against the yew. 'I'm not scared of you,' she told the shadows. Her voice sounded reedy and unconvincing.

Moments later, Torak and Wolf returned. Wolf raced to snuffle furiously at Renn's things. Torak's jaw dropped.

'I saw something at the lake,' she told him. 'Then this.'

'What did you see?'

'It had pale hair. It looked angry.'

He flinched.

'Do you know what it is?' she said.

'No, I – no.' He started searching for tracks, but the light was almost gone, and he didn't find any. 'Either it knows how to cover its tracks,' he said, 'or it doesn't leave any.'

'What do you mean? Torak, what *is* it?'

He chewed his lip. Then he stood up. 'Whatever it is, we're not sleeping on the ground.'

The yew didn't like being climbed. It choked them in clouds of pollen and tried to evade their grip by shedding bark. Twice, a branch whipped round and tried to throw them off. They were scratched and exhausted by the time they'd settled in its arms.

'The wind's getting up,' said Torak. 'We'd better tie ourselves to the trunk.'

Renn hung their damp, gritty sleeping-sacks to dry, and

peered down into the gloom. She saw Wolf silently pacing. She said, 'Let's hope Wolf and the ravens warn us of danger.'

Wolf ran in circles round the yew, bristling with disapproval. He *hated* it when the taillesses climbed trees. Why did they do this?

Normal wolves do not climb trees. And normal wolves *like* the Dark, it's their best time, when they run about and play. They do not curl up and sleep for ever.

Wolf hated it here. The Forest felt different. The trees were too alert and the smells were all mixed up. Some of the trees smelt of earth, while the taillesses who lived here smelt of trees. They were angry and scared, and although each pack had quite a big range, they fought; Wolf didn't know why. Worse still, Tall Tailless and the pack-sister had changed their overpelts and even their smells, so that Wolf hardly knew them.

His sleeps were troubled by the scratching of demon claws and the cries of eagle owls, and sometimes when he woke up, he caught the nose-biting scent of the tailless who smelt of the Bright Beast. This tailless worried Wolf a lot, because its mind was broken, so he couldn't sense what it wanted.

The scent of the broken-minded tailless was thick in Wolf's nose as he prowled the yew's roots, but he sensed that the tailless itself was gone. Maybe it also climbed trees. Wolf decided to stay close, in case it came back.

In the Up, the Bright White Eye was half-open, sleepily watching over her many little cubs. Wolf stalked a weasel, but it got away. He caught a moth, but it made him sneeze, so he spat it out. And still the taillesses slept.

Suddenly, Wolf pricked his ears. Further down the valley, the ravens were cawing. They'd found a roe deer which was Not-Breath, they wanted Wolf to come and rip it open, so that they could feed.

Wolf wondered what to do. He had to stay and guard the taillesses.

But he was hungry.

THIRTEEN

As night deepened, the other inhabitants of the Forest emerged.

Bats flitted from hollows in the yew. A grey owl settled on the end of Torak's branch, its body swaying, its moonlit eyes fixed on his. He stared back till it flew away.

It was a blustery night and the trees were wide awake.

So was he.

Who – or what – had attacked Renn's gear? Was it Bale's vengeful spirit, or something else? *An ash-haired hunter burning inside.* Saeunn's prophecy could mean anything.

Straining at the rope that bound him to the trunk, he twisted round to see if Renn was awake on the other side. She was curled up like a squirrel, fast asleep.

He ached to be on the move. Somewhere in these secret valleys, Thiazzi was hiding; and the trail was getting cold.

Not even Wolf could follow it much longer.

On the ground, branches rustled as something large pushed its way through. Torak couldn't see anything, but as the creature drew nearer, he heard munching and huffing breath. Then a darkness like a walking boulder passed beneath him. He glimpsed massive, humped shoulders; an enormous head with short, half-moon horns.

Bison.

He watched the creature lean against the yew's trunk and give itself a luxurious scratching that made the whole tree shiver. Then, with a deep, satisfied grunt, it ambled off.

Soon afterwards, Torak caught the familiar tail-swish of horses. As the herd moved beneath him, he glimpsed a wobbly foal duck beneath its mother's belly to suckle; a young mare nibble-grooming the mane of an older one whose scarred rump showed her to be the survivor of many a hunt. He felt a settling of awe. Unlike the dun-coloured horses of the Open Forest, these were as black as a moonless night.

Renn mumbled in her sleep, and the lead mare jerked up her head. The sacred herd melted into the darkness like a dream.

The Forest felt lonely after they'd gone. Torak wished Wolf and the ravens would return.

The wind strengthened and the trees creaked and moaned. He wondered what they were saying. If he knew their speech, they could tell him where to find Thiazzi.

The thought dropped into his mind like a pebble into a Forest pool. *Become one of them. Spirit walk.*

He wondered if he dared. Trees are the most mysterious of beings. They harbour fire and give life to all, yet eat only sunlight. Alone among creatures, they grow a new limb when one is lost. Some never sleep, while others slumber naked through the cruellest winter. They witness the scurrying lives of hunters and prey, but keep their own thoughts hidden.

Torak wrenched open his medicine pouch and sought the piece of black root he'd kept secret even from Renn. Saeunn had given it to him. *For when you need it*, she'd said.

He chewed fast. Bitterness flooded his mouth. The root was potent. Before he'd swallowed it, a sharp pain pierced his guts. Waves of cramp took hold, and he doubled up, the rope cutting into his midriff. He began to be afraid. He should wake Renn. But the rawhide held him. He couldn't reach.

The cramps were coming faster, a relentless tide sucking at his souls. He opened his mouth to call Renn's name . . .

. . . and his voice was the groaning of bark and the roaring of branches. His twig-fingers knew the chill moonlight and the wind's screaming caress, his boughs the scratch of wasp and the weight of sleeping boy and girl. Deep in the earth, his roots knew the burrowing moles and the soft, blind worms, and all was good, for he was *tree*, and he rejoiced in the wildness of the night.

Lost in the coursing tree-blood, the speck of spirit that was Torak begged it to tell him where to find Thiazzi. The yew gave a sigh and lifted him out into the night.

Helpless as a spark borne by a rushing wind, Torak was carried through the Forest on a soughing sea of voices, from yew to holly, from seedling to sapling to mighty oak, faster than wolf can lope or raven fly. Terror seized him. Too far, he thought, you'll never get back!

When at last he came to rest, his tree-fingers knew the icy winds sweeping down from the High Mountains. He was in the golden tree-blood of another yew, but this one was old beyond imagining, ancient as the Forest itself. His boughs speared stars, his roots split stone and trapped demons in the Otherworld. His limbs sheltered owl and marten, squirrel and bat. To the creatures who dwelt in him, he was the world, but to the Great Yew their lives were as brief as the trembling of a leaf, and long after they were gone, he would endure.

Lost in the vast awareness, Torak felt the prick of tokoroth claws on his bark. He heard demons howling for the fiery stone that was almost within their reach. Flames seared his branches. He sensed the Oak Mage circling, chanting spells.

The Oak Mage raised his arms to the sky. *I am the truth and the Way. I am master of fire. I am ruler of the Forest!*

The wind rose and the voice of the Great Yew rose with it. Torak was drowning in voices, all the trees of the Forest rising, swelling to an obliterating roar, tearing him apart . . .

'Torak!' whispered Renn. 'Torak! Wake up!'

His head turned, but she could see that he didn't know her. His eyes were empty and unseeing, no souls inside.

No souls. He was spirit walking.

He had woken her by wrenching himself free from the rope, and now he knelt on his branch, swaying, muttering. She was terrifed that he would step into nothingness and break his neck.

She edged round to his side of the trunk. He was out of reach. She stayed where she was, afraid of startling him.

At last he spoke, in a hollow voice that was not his own. 'I am the Great Yew,' he told the rushing wind. 'I am older than the Forest. I began amid the roots of the First Tree. I was seedling when the last snows of the Long Cold melted into the earth; sapling at the coming of the Wave. I have never known sleep. But I have known anger . . . '

Renn didn't know what to do. Her Magecraft wasn't strong enough to call back his souls. Praying to the guardian, she stretched out her hand.

Torak rose on his branch and began to walk.

Pain jolted him awake: a raven beak, tugging at his earlobe.

He was dizzy. The wind was blowing in his face, the trees roaring in his head.

'Torak!' Renn's voice came to him from far away. 'Torak, look at me. Only at me. *Don't move!*'

The raven lifted off his shoulder and he staggered. Beneath him, the ground swayed.

Not the ground. *The branch.* He stood on the end of the branch, his hands clawing empty air.

'Look at me,' commanded Renn. She crouched near the bole of the tree, one hand gripping the rope that circled the trunk, the other straining towards him. *'Do not look down.'*

He looked down. A dizzying drop. Far below, on the yew's snake-like roots, something squatted. He saw ashen hair and a pale, upturned face. He swayed.

Renn's voice called him back. 'Torak. Come – to – me.' Her dark eyes drew him.

He sank to his knees and crawled towards her.

'You don't remember *anything*?' said Renn.

Torak shook his head. He was shaking and sick, worse than she'd ever seen him. It had been all she could do to get him down from the tree.

'Not untying the rope or crawling onto the branch? Nothing?'

'Nothing,' he mumbled.

At last she got the waterskin open. 'Here. You'll feel better.'

He didn't respond. He sat with his back against the yew, staring into its branches.

The wind had dropped, and dawn was coming. Rip and Rek perched in the lower boughs, sleeping off the horse meat Renn had given them to say thank you. She doubted if Torak even saw them. There was a strange, shattered light in his eyes, and when she looked closer, she saw that they were no longer a pure light-grey. In their depths were tiny flecks of green.

'I saw him,' he said. 'I saw Thiazzi. He's near the Mountains. Making spells. He thinks he can rule the Forest.' He rolled onto all fours and retched.

When it was over, he collapsed against the tree. 'I thought I'd never get back.'

'What do you mean?'

He shut his eyes. 'When you spirit walk in a raven – or a bear or an elk – you stay in that creature. But the trees – they're not separate. For them, thinking, talking, spirit walking, it's all the same thing. From tree to tree, ash to beech to holly, it passes between them. Faster, further, than you could ever imagine.' He clutched his temples. 'So many *voices*!

Renn could only watch helplessly. What worried her most was that this time, while he was spirit walking, his body had moved. That had never happened before.

She knew that people do sometimes sleepwalk, if their name-soul slips out during a dream. The body wanders, trying to find the errant soul, and usually they get back together before either has left the shelter. But she had no idea what this might mean for Torak.

'Why did you do it, Torak? Why spirit walk now?'

He opened his eyes. 'To find Thiazzi.' He hesitated. 'I see him, Renn. Sometimes it's a flash of fair hair. Sometimes he's right there. Streaming wet. Accusing.'

A chill crawled over her skin. She saw from his face that he meant Bale.

She thought of the day of the death rites, when Torak had stood on the beach and shouted Bale's name to the sky. As if he'd *wanted* to be haunted. 'Why would he be accusing?' she said.

He struck the back of his head against the yew, hard enough to hurt. 'We had a fight. I went off on my own.'

Oh, Torak. 'What – what did you fight about?'

He avoided her gaze. 'He was going to ask you to stay with him.'

Renn felt the heat rising to her face.

'He didn't want to quarrel,' Torak went on. 'It was me. I was the one. I left him to keep watch alone. That's why he was killed.'

Around them, the birds were waking up. Renn saw the dew glistening on fat caterpillar curls of bracken. A bumblebee bumping about among the windflowers.

All this suffering, she thought. Bale dead. His whole clan grieving. Fin-Kedinn hurt. Torak tormented by guilt. All because of Thiazzi. Until now, she hadn't grasped how the evil of the Soul-Eaters spread, like cracks on a frozen lake.

'Torak,' she said at last. 'That doesn't make it your fault. Thiazzi's the killer. Not you.'

The bee settled on Torak's knee, and he watched its unsteady progress. 'Then why is he haunting me? I have to fulfil my oath, Renn. Or he'll be with me for ever.'

She thought about that. 'Maybe you're right. But I'll be with you too. And Wolf. And Rip and Rek.' She paused. 'Only from now on, *don't* tell me to go back to my clan.'

His lip curled. Then he snorted. Easing the bee onto his palm, he placed it on a dock leaf.

Dawn came, and they sat side by side, watching sunlight slanting through the Forest.

After a while, Torak said, 'If he had asked you to stay with him, would you have said yes?'

Renn turned to stare at him. 'How can you ask that?' she said, exasperated.

He was puzzled. 'I'm sorry, I . . . Does that mean no?'

She opened her mouth to reply, but at that moment, Wolf returned, his muzzle dark with blood. Giving them both a carrion-smelling greeting, he licked Torak under the chin, and they exchanged one of their speaking glances.

Renn asked him what Wolf was saying.

'Bright Beast,' he told her. 'And – I'm not sure, something broken. Think? Mind? Broken mind?'

'Mad,' they said together.

They never had time to wonder what it meant.

Wolf broke into an odd, excited little whimper and shot off into the undergrowth. Torak pulled Renn to her feet and moved in front of her. Five silent hunters came out from the trees. In the time it took Renn to draw her knife, they were surrounded. The hunters were clad in plain buckskin and carried no weapons. Somehow, they didn't need them. Renn saw that they wore no headbands. Whose side were they on?

'You will come with us,' said a quiet voice which was used to being obeyed. 'Your search is at an end.'

FOURTEEN

The woman wore a necklet of beechnuts and a remote expression, as if her thoughts were on matters no-one else could understand.

Renn guessed she was the Mage or Leader, or both. Her long brown hair was loose, except for a lock at the temple, matted with earthblood; and from her belt hung an antler tine. The clan-tattoo on her forehead was a small, black, cloven hoof.

'You're Red Deer,' said Renn.

'And you're Raven,' said the woman, calmly seeing through her disguise. 'And you,' she turned to Torak, 'are the spirit walker.'

He gaped. 'How did you know?'

'We felt your souls walk. You can mask it from others, but not from the Red Deer.'

'He doesn't mask it,' said Renn.

'Then someone does it for him,' the woman replied.

Renn wanted to ask what she meant, but Torak said eagerly, 'My mother was Red Deer. Did you know her?'

'Of course.'

He took a breath that ended in a gulp. 'What was she like?'

'Not here,' said the woman. 'We'll take you to our camp.'

There was a gesture of protest from one of her companions, a man whose hair was hidden by a binding of reddish bark. 'But Durrain, they're outsiders! They shouldn't see our camp, especially not the girl!'

'I'm not an outsider,' said Torak, 'I'm kin.'

'What have you got against me?' said Renn.

'We will go to camp,' repeated Durrain. Then to Torak and Renn, 'You may keep your weapons, but you won't need them. While you're with the Red Deer, you'll be quite safe.'

Renn felt that she spoke the truth – after all, Fin-Kedinn had said to seek them out – but she didn't like Durrain. Her thin face was as unfeeling as stone. And she hadn't even asked their names.

Durrain led them east, on a deer trail which kept to the thickets. Twice, Renn spotted Wolf, staying level with them. She wondered what he thought of their turning away from Thiazzi's scent trail, but when she mentioned this to Torak, he brushed it aside. 'Durrain said she'd help us.'

'She said our search was at an end. That might not mean the same thing.'

'They're my bone kin. They *have* to help.'

Pushing through the thickets was hard work, and a handsome young hunter offered to carry Renn's sleeping-sack. She declined, then wished she hadn't. The hunter guessed, and carried it anyway.

She pointed to the man with the bark-bound head, who was walking in front. 'Why doesn't he like me?'

The young man sighed. 'We fostered a Raven once. He helped the Soul-Eater make the demon bear.'

Renn bridled. 'That was my brother. The Soul-Eater tricked him, too.'

The man with the bark-bound head glared at her. 'So *you* say. The bear killed my mate. That's why I don't like Ravens.'

When he was out of earshot, the young hunter apologized. 'He still misses her.'

'Is that why he binds his head?' asked Renn.

'Yes, we place our dead in their chosen tree, then bind our heads in its bark, to remember.'

'But you don't wear headbands. So whose side are you on?'

He drew himself up. 'We take no sides. We never fight.'

Renn raised her eyebrows. 'What do the other clans think of that?'

'They scorn us, but they leave us alone.'

For now, she thought. She glanced at Torak, but he wasn't listening. He was drinking in every detail of his mother's clan, his face full of longing. Renn felt a twist of worry. She hoped these strange, distant people didn't let him down.

They walked for most of the day, and Renn soon lost her bearings. At last they reached a lake with a wooded islet in the middle. She was told it was Lake Blackwater, amid surprise that she didn't already know.

The Red Deer camp lay above the lake, and was so well concealed that she would have passed it if it hadn't been for the fire. A mound of juniper turned out to be the biggest shelter she'd ever seen: she counted seven doorways covered by reindeer-hide flaps stained green. A couple of dogs – the first she'd encountered in the Deep Forest – came to investigate, caught Wolf's scent on her, and fled. Children peered out, then ducked inside.

It was weirdly quiet, but for the first time in days, she felt safe. Nothing could get her here: neither tokoroths, nor Forest Horse hunters, nor the ash-haired menace. The fabled Magecraft of the Red Deer kept them at bay. And yet all she could see were a few tiny bark bundles tied to trees.

The young hunter led Torak to the lake to wash, and a woman beckoned Renn to a secluded bay. After some persuasion, she stripped and stood shivering while the woman used a cake of what appeared to be hard grey mud to scrub off her Deep Forest disguise. It was good to be herself again, but her skin stung. She asked what was in the grey cake.

The woman was surprised she didn't know. 'It's ash. We burn green bracken, then mix it with water and bake it.'

Ash, thought Renn. Always ash.

'Everyone in the Deep Forest uses it,' said the woman. 'It's like soapwort, but better.'

Another woman brought clothes: leggings and jerkin of roe deer buckskin lined with hare fur, neat elkhide boots, and a supple, hooded cape which Renn mistook for wovenbark, but was told was nettlestem. Everything fitted, but she was upset to learn that apart from her clan-creature feathers, her Raven clothes had been burnt.

'But ours are so much better,' protested the women.

Better clothes, better washing, better everything, Renn thought crossly. Maybe we should all give up and imitate them.

To boost her spirits, she pretended she had to go to the midden, and when she was alone, she rolled up one legging, took the beaver-tooth knife the Otter Clan had given her, and tied it to her calf with her spare bowstring. There. Just in case.

When she got back, Torak was sitting by the fire, also in new clothes, and scrubbed of his disguise. It was a relief to see him looking himself again; but they'd taken away his headband, and he kept touching his outcast tattoo.

He made room for her beside him while the rest of the clan settled round the fire. 'Stop scowling,' he whispered, 'they're helping us. And smell that food!'

She snorted. 'It's bound to be *so* much better than ours.'

But she had to admit it was good. A huge wovenroot basket had been hung directly over the embers. It was full of a fragrant stew of chopped auroch meat, mushrooms and bracken tops, which was cooked when the basket was nearly burnt through. There were also delicious flatcakes of crushed hazelnuts and pine pollen, and a big pail of honey to ladle over everything, with steaming spruce-needle tea to wash it all down.

It was wonderful to roast by a fire again, but apart from a brief prayer to the Forest, the Red Deer ate in silence. Renn thought with a pang of the Ravens' noisy nightmeals, with everyone swapping hunting stories.

As soon as they'd finished, Durrain began to question Torak. Surprisingly, she showed no interest in why they had come; she only wanted to know what it was like to spirit walk in a tree.

Torak struggled to explain. 'I – I was a yew. Then I was in tree after tree. Too many voices . . . I couldn't bear it.'

'Ah,' sighed the whole clan.

Even Durrain betrayed a flicker of emotion. 'What you heard was the Voice of the Forest. All the trees that are, or have ever been. It's too vast for men to bear. If you'd heard it for more than a heartbeat, your souls would have been torn apart. And yet – how I envy you.'

Torak swallowed. 'My mother . . . You said you knew her. Tell me about her?'

Durrain dismissed that with a wave of her hand. 'She chose to leave. I can tell you nothing.'

'Nothing?' Torak was aghast.

Renn felt angry for him. 'Surely you tried to find her?'

Durrain gave her a chilly smile.

'But – she and Torak's father were fighting the Soul-Eaters. They needed your help.'

'The Red Deer never fight,' said Durrain. Her eyes were a vivid beechnut brown, and they pierced Renn's souls. 'I see that you have some small skill at Magecraft. In the Deep Forest you're out of your depth. You are no Mage.'

She was right. It was Renn's turn to be crushed.

Beside her, Torak stirred. 'You don't know anything about Renn. Last summer, her visions warned us of the flood. She saved whole clans.'

'Indeed,' said Durrain.

Torak lifted his chin. 'We're wasting time. You said our search is at an end. Do you know where the Oak Mage is?'

'There is no Oak Mage in the Deep Forest,' declared Durrain.

'You're wrong,' said Torak. 'We tracked him here. The trail leads south.'

'If there was a Soul-Eater in the Deep Forest, the Red

Deer would know it.'

'You didn't before,' said Renn. 'The crippled wanderer lived with you for a whole summer and you never knew who he was.'

That drew angry murmurs from the others, and Durrain's lips thinned. 'Your search is at an end. Tonight we will pray. Tomorrow we'll take you back to the Open Forest.'

'No!' cried Renn and Torak together.

'You don't understand what you've blundered into,' said Durrain. 'The Deep Forest is at war!'

'But you never fight,' retorted Renn, 'so why should that affect you?'

'It affects us all,' said Durrain. 'It keeps the World Spirit away, which blights the Forest. Surely even in the Open Forest you know of this?'

'No, we're much too ignorant,' said Renn, 'why don't you enlighten us?'

Durrain flashed her an angry look. 'In winter the World Spirit haunts the fells as a willow-haired woman. In summer it walks the deep woods as a tall man with the antlers of a stag. This much you know?'

Renn made a huge effort to hold onto her temper.

'In spring, at the moment of turning, the Great Oak in the sacred grove bursts into leaf. Not this spring. The buds have been eaten by demons. The Spirit hasn't come.' She paused. 'We've tried everything.'

'The red branches,' said Torak.

Durrain nodded. 'Each clan beseeches the Spirit in its own way. The Aurochs paint branches. Lynx and Bat make sacrifices. The Forest Horses also paint branches, and their new Mage fasts alone in the sacred grove, seeking a sign.'

Renn felt Torak stiffen. 'The Forest Horse Mage,' he

said. 'Is that a man or a woman?'

'A man,' said Durrain.

Renn's heart began to race. 'What does he look like?'

'No-one sees his face. At all times, he wears a mask of wood, to be one with the trees.'

'Where is the sacred grove?' said Torak.

'In the valley of the horses,' said Durrain.

'Where's that?' said Renn.

'We never tell outsiders.'

'In whose range is it?' said Torak, 'Auroch or Forest Horse?'

'The sacred grove is the heart of the Forest,' said Durrain. 'It belongs to no-one. All may go there, though only in greatest need. At least, this was the way until the Forest Horse Mage forbade it.'

Renn took a deep breath. 'What if we told you that the Forest Horse Mage is Thiazzi in disguise?'

Durrain gave her a pitying stare, while the others smiled in disbelief.

'But if we're right,' said Torak, 'you'd help us? You'd help me, your bone kin, fight the Soul-Eater?'

'The Red Deer never fight,' repeated Durrain.

'But you can't do nothing!' cried Renn.

'We pray for the fighting to stop,' retorted Durrain. 'We pray for the World Spirit to come.'

'That's your answer?' said Torak. 'To pray?'

Durrain rose to her feet. 'I'll show you why we do not fight,' she said, spitting out her words like pebbles. Seizing Torak and Renn by the wrist, she dragged them out of camp.

They headed uphill, and soon reached a small glade where the evening sun glowed in drifts of yellow hawkbit. There was no birdsong. The glade was eerily quiet. In the middle, Renn saw a tangle of bleached bones: the skeletons of two red deer stags.

It was horribly easy to guess what had happened. Last autumn's rut, and the stags had fought over females. Renn saw the great heads clashing, the antlers locking. The struggle to untangle themselves. They couldn't. They were trapped.

'*This* is the sign the Spirit sent,' said Durrain. 'See what befell our clan-creatures! They fought. They couldn't get free. They starved to death. *This* is what happens when you fight. *This* is why the Red Deer will have *none* of it!'

FIFTEEN

As Durrain led them back to camp, Torak hung back, and Renn fell into step beside him. 'Are you all right?' she said.

'Fine.'

She touched his hand. 'I know you hoped for more from them.'

He forced a shrug. Because she was Renn, he didn't mind her feeling sorry for him, but to stop her saying anything else he said, 'I think they're wrong about not fighting.'

'Me too.'

'How can you not fight Soul-Eaters? If nobody fought them they'd take over the Forest.'

'Although,' she said, mimicking Durrain's lofty tones, 'who are *we* to question the ways of the Red Deer?'

He grinned. 'Especially not you, you ignorant Raven.'

She jabbed her elbow in his ribs and he yelped, earning a disapproving glance from Durrain.

As they neared the camp, Torak said in a low voice, 'But they have told us something important.'

Renn nodded. 'We need to find the sacred grove.'

Dusk was falling, and most of the Red Deer had gone into the shelter. Durrain was waiting for them. 'We pray till dawn,' she announced. 'You will pray with us.'

Renn tried to look obedient, and Torak bowed, although he had no intention of praying. He wasn't going to be distracted any longer.

A woman emerged from an adjoining trail, spotted Durrain, and dithered, as if wondering where to hide.

Durrain heaved a sigh. 'Where have you been?'

'I – I took an offering to the horses,' stammered the woman.

'You should have told me first.'

'Yes, Mage,' the woman said humbly.

Torak caught Renn's eye. *The horses.*

To give him a chance to tackle the woman, she asked Durrain to explain how the Red Deer went into a trance. The Mage gave her a look, and took her into the shelter.

'We should go in,' bleated the woman. She had flaky skin which reminded Torak of dried reindeer meat, and she kept blinking as if anticipating a blow. Her bark head-binding was filthy and needed replacing.

To set her at ease, he asked whom she mourned.

'M-my child,' she mumbled. 'We should go in.'

'And you make offerings to the horses? In their valley?'

'The Windriver, yes.' She gestured behind her, then clapped her hand to her mouth. 'We should go *in!*'

Simmering with excitement, Torak left his axe and bow

where he could find them, and followed her in. It was almost too easy.

Inside, it was as dim as the Forest at Midsummer. From the cross-beams, thousands of nettle fibres hung to dry: they brushed his face like long green hair. Men and women sat on opposite sides with Durrain in the middle, cradling a pair of deer-hoof rattles. There was no fire. The only warmth was the dank heat of breath.

Torak made out Renn, who gave him a conspiratorial smile. He felt guilty, because she wasn't coming with him. He couldn't have said why; he just knew that when he confronted Thiazzi, she mustn't be there to see it.

Making his way to the men's side, he found a place in front of one of the doorways.

The last Red Deer crawled in and set a bowl and a platter before Durrain. She lifted the bowl and drank. 'Rain from the tracks of the tree-headed guardian,' she intoned. 'Drink the wisdom of the Forest.' She handed on the bowl.

From the platter she took a piece of flatcake. 'Bark of the ever-watchful pine. Eat the wisdom of the Forest.'

When it was Torak's turn, he hid the flatcake up his sleeve and only pretended to sip from the bowl. Surreptitiously, he put out his hand, and felt cool air beneath the hide flap.

Durrain's gaze raked the throng.

He froze.

Durrain began shaking the rattles in a steady, cantering rhythm. 'Forest,' she chanted, 'You see all. You know all. Not a swallow falls, not a bat breathes, but you know it. Hear us.'

'Hear us,' echoed the others.

'End the strife between the clans. Bring the stag-headed Spirit back to your sacred valleys.'

On and on went the chanting and the galloping hooves, and still Durrain watched her people. Middle-night came and went. Torak had almost given up hope, when, without breaking rhythm, she cast her hood over her face – and the others did the same.

As the Red Deer chanted themselves deeper into the trance, Torak backed closer to the flap. The men flanking him were lost in their wovenstem darkness. They didn't see him escape.

Grabbing his weapons, he headed up the trail.

He hadn't gone far when Rip and Rek swooped and gave him a welcoming caw. *Where have you been?*

Wolf appeared like a grey shadow and ran at his side. *Bitten One. Not far.*

The half-eaten moon was setting, dawn was not far off. Torak quickened his pace. The thrill of the chase fizzed in his blood. He felt swift and invincible, a hunter closing on his prey. This was meant to be.

The boy escapes. This was meant to be.

For three days and nights the Chosen One has watched the unbelievers, as the Master willed. The girl drains the power from a curse stick as easily as pouring water from a pail. The boy summons ravens from the sky and speaks with the great grey wolf – and his spirit walks.

The boy believes he is cunning, tracking the Master to the sacred grove. No-one tracks the Master. The Master summons, and others obey. Even the fire obeys the Master.

The will of the Master must be done.

SIXTEEN

Dawn had broken, and neither the Red Deer nor Renn came after him. Torak almost wished they would. Soon, nothing would stand between him and his vengeance.

As the day wore on, he followed the trail up the Windriver, although this swift brown torrent bore scant resemblance to the mighty river it would become in the Open Forest.

Wolf padded at his side with drooping tail and lowered head. Even the ravens had stopped swooping after butterflies. The thrill of the hunt had given way to apprehension.

The valley narrowed to a gorge and the river became a rushing stream. A dry south wind had been blowing all day, but now it dropped to a whisper. Torak felt a tingling in his spine. They were entering the foothills of the High Mountains.

Wolf sniffed a clod of earth that had been kicked up by a horse's hoof. Torak stooped for a long black tail-hair. Above him, the new leaves of beech and birch glowed a brilliant green. Blackthorn blossom glittered like snow. The air was fresh with the scent of spruce, and alive with birdsong: chaffinch, warbler, thrush, wren. Even the speedwell on the trail was a preternatural blue, like flowers in a dream. He had reached the valley of the horses.

Wolf raised his head. *Do we go on?*

I must, Torak told him. *Not you. Dangerous.*

If you must, I must.

They walked on in the flickering shade.

The trail, Torak noticed, had been trodden by many hooves and paws, but no boots. The prey showed no fear of him, and he guessed that here, people were forbidden to hunt. A black woodpecker hopped backwards along a branch, probing for ants. It was so close that Torak glimpsed its long grey tongue. A roe buck munched deadnettle. He could have touched its coarse brown fur. He came upon a boar snuffling for roots; she watched him pass without raising her snout.

The valley narrowed to a gorge, and birch gave way to mossy spruce. The breeze died. The birds fell silent. Torak's footfalls sounded loud. He touched his shoulder, where his clan-creature skin used to be. A knot of dread tightened under his heart.

Ever since Bale's death, his whole purpose had been to find Thiazzi. He hadn't thought about what came after. He did now. He had to kill the strongest man in the Forest.

He had to kill a man.

Perhaps this was why he'd left Renn behind: because he

113

didn't want her to see him do it. But he missed her.

A murmur of wings behind him and he turned, hoping it was Rip and Rek. It was a sparrowhawk on a stump, plucking the breast of a headless thrush.

Maybe, thought Torak, the ravens have gone because they know what I'm going to do.

But Wolf was still with him. He was gazing at Torak, and his amber eyes held the pure, steady light of the guide. *Do not go on.*

I must, Torak replied.

This is bad.

I know. I must.

The sun sank lower and the trees closed in. The river disappeared, but Torak heard it echoing underground. Finally, its voice fell to nothing.

A stone clattered behind him. When it came to rest, the stillness surged back like something alive.

The trail rounded a bend and the Mountains reared before him, startlingly close. The valley walls leaned in, shutting out the dying light. Ahead, the tallest holly trees he'd ever seen warded him back. Beyond them, he knew, lay the sacred grove: the heart of the Forest.

Some places hold an echo of events; others possess their own spirit. Torak sensed the spirit of this place as a soundless humming in his bones. From his pouch, he drew his mother's medicine horn. He shook earthblood into his palm and daubed some on his cheeks and brow. The horn seemed to vibrate, like the humming in his marrow.

Wolf nosed his hand. His ears were flat against his skull. He was no longer the guide. He was Torak's pack-brother, and frightened.

Torak knelt and blew gently on his muzzle, feeling the tickle of his whiskers and breathing his sweet, clean smell.

He couldn't let Wolf come any further. It was too dangerous. He had to do this alone. Hating the confusion he would cause, he told Wolf to go.

Wolf refused.

Torak repeated the command.

Wolf ran in a circle. *You must not hunt the Bitten One!*

Go, Torak replied.

Wolf pawed his knee. *Danger!* Uff!

Torak hardened his heart. *Go!*

Wolf gave an anxious whimper and raced off into the Forest.

So now you're alone, thought Torak. He felt the chill of the night seeping out of the earth. He rose and walked into the dark beneath the trees.

As Wolf raced up the slope, worry and fear fought within him. This was a terrible place. The holly trees whispered warnings he didn't understand. They were very old, and they didn't want him here.

He reached a ridge above the whispering trees and skittered to a halt. The breeze carried a tangle of scents to his nose. He smelt the Bright Beast-that-Bites-Hot, and the Bitten One, and a whiff of demon. He smelt his pack-brother's fear and his blood-hunger. This was not the hunger of the hunt, it was deeper, fiercer. It was not-wolf. Wolf didn't understand it, but he feared it. And he feared for Tall Tailless, because he felt in his fur that if Tall Tailless attacked the Bitten One, he would be killed.

The Bitten One was stronger than a bear. Not even the Bright Beast dared attack him. What could one wolf do?

Wolf trotted up and down the ridge, mewing in distress.

He felt a faint shudder in the earth. He swivelled his ears. Loping to the top of the ridge, he leapt onto a log. He caught the rich scent of the huge prey that is like auroch – but not.

He smelt that a herd of these not-aurochs was feeding in the next valley. They were enormous creatures, but timid, although they could be extremely bad-tempered, and hated being chased, as Wolf had learnt the previous Dark.

He raced off to find them.

The holly trees smelt of dust and spiders. Their vigilance pressed upon Torak, drawing the breath from his lungs as the wind draws smoke from a shelter.

Eventually, the hollies thinned, and between their straight black trunks he saw the red glimmer of a fire. He drew his knife. As he went closer, he heard the crackle of flames. He caught the stink of charred flesh.

He reached the last tree and edged behind it. The holly's bark felt cold as slate beneath his palm.

The sacred grove was washed in blue moonlight, and shadowed by the broken shoulders of the Mountains. A circle of raked embers smouldered on stony ground. Beyond it, hazed by smoke, two enormous trees stood side by side, their upper branches intertwining like hands.

The Great Oak pushed skywards in eternal struggle. Its mighty trunk was furrowed like an ice river, and in the uncertain light, Torak saw gnarled bark faces glaring at him. No leaves softened the oak's twig fingers: its buds had been gnawed by demons. But from some branches hung small, lumpy shapes. Torak couldn't see what they were. He dreaded finding out.

The Great Yew was ancient beyond imagining. Torak knew, because he had walked in its deep green souls. Its twisted limbs were weathered to a driftwood silver, but underneath, the golden sapwood pulsed. Its ever-wakeful boughs had survived fire and flood, lightning and drought. Its roots were harder than stone, and held down the Mountains. The Great Yew feared nothing, not even demons.

From nowhere, a gust of wind cleared the smoke and breathed life into the fire. Torak saw that a stake had been driven into its heart, and from this hung a slender, blackened carcass.

Torak felt sick. Now he understood what dangled from the Great Oak. Carcasses. Too small to be human, too charred to be recognizable.

To murder a hunter. He remembered the Soul-Eaters' dreadful sacrifices in the caves of the Far North. He remembered Fin-Kedinn telling of the bad times long ago, when the clans had killed hunters, including people.

This, he thought, is evil. He could feel it in the air: a rotten, choking sickness, palsying the heart of the Forest.

His hand on his knife-hilt was slippery with sweat. There was no turning back. He had to leave the shelter of the holly trees and find Thiazzi.

He was about to take the first step when one of the rocks beyond the fire rose, spread its arms and became a man.

SEVENTEEN

The Mage rose from the very roots of the sacred grove. He wore a mantle of flowing horsehide and a long, graven mask crested with a mane of horsetails. Painted eyes glared scarlet, and the gaping mouth was fringed with black feathers that shuddered at every breath.

Spirit breath, Renn had told Torak once. *A mask is a spirit's face. When you put on a mask, you become that spirit. The feathers show that the spirit lives.*

Mask and mantle declared him to be the Forest Horse Mage, but upon his breast he wore a wreath of acorns and mistletoe, the tokens of his true clan, and from it hung a small, heavy pouch. The fire-opal.

Behind the holly tree, Torak clumsily sheathed his knife. It would be useless against such power. He unslung his bow and fumbled in his quiver for an arrow. His heart was pounding so hard that it hurt. He felt like a mouse about to attack an auroch.

Standing before the fire, the Mage began to pant, forcing the air from his chest in harsh exhalations, ugh – ugh – ugh. He stepped closer to the fire. He stepped *into* it. Through the shimmering heat, Torak watched his naked feet tread the living embers. Not possible, he thought.

Panting faster, ugh ugh ugh, the Mage snatched the carcass from the stake and walked back to solid ground.

Torak's head reeled. If not even fire could harm him . . . He couldn't do this. He couldn't do it.

He watched the Mage raise a fallen spruce tree as if it were a twig, and set it against the trunk of the Great Oak. The spruce was notched to make a ladder. The Mage ascended and hung the carcass from a bough. Descending, he took a sack from among the roots of the Great Oak and drew out a hawk.

Torak's belly turned over. The hawk was alive. It fluttered wildly as the Mage tied it by one leg to a stake.

Again the Mage began those harsh, panting breaths. But this time, as he raised the stake, his mantle fell away from his forearms, and Torak saw his three-fingered hand and his Oak Clan tattoo. The skin was scored with angry scabs. Torak thought of Bale, clawing his attacker as he fought for life. His souls hardened. It was time to fulfil his oath.

Wiping his palms on his leggings, he nocked the arrow to his bow. He would move away from the tree, into full view. He would shout the challenge, give Thiazzi a chance to seize his weapons. And then . . .

The Soul-Eater carried his fluttering burden into the fire, planted the stake and walked away.

Torak couldn't bear it. He took aim and let fly. The

hawk hung dead, the arrow quivering in its breast.

Slowly, the Mage took off his mask and placed it on the ground. He turned, and Torak saw him at last. The russet mane, the thicket of beard. The face as hard as sun-cracked earth. The pitiless green eyes.

'So, Spirit Walker. You obeyed my summons.'

Torak stepped out from behind the tree. 'Take up your weapons, Thiazzi. You killed my kinsman. Now I'm going to kill you.'

EIGHTEEN

Torak faced Thiazzi across ten paces of drifting smoke. 'You won't get away from me this time,' he said, nocking another arrow to his bow.

The Oak Mage threw back his head and laughed. 'I, get away from *you*? You're here because I want you here!' Flicking his mantle behind his shoulders, he brandished a whip in one hand, an axe in the other. The lash was coiled like a viper. The axe was the largest Torak had ever seen.

'I wondered who dared follow me from the islands,' said Thiazzi, slicing the air with deft twists of his wrist, 'so I sent my minion to find out. Since you entered my Forest, I've known every step you've taken, every breath you've drawn. Now it ends.'

'You won't find it that easy,' said Torak, edging sideways round the fire. 'I could have killed you in the Far North.

121

Remember?'

The whip cracked, wrenching Torak's bow from his hand. 'My power is greater than yours!' spat Thiazzi, tossing the bow in the flames. 'See, even the fire obeys me!'

Smoke wafted across Torak's sight. When it cleared, Thiazzi stood no more than two paces from him.

'But since the World Spirit has delivered you into my hands,' the Oak Mage went on, 'I shall add your power to my own.'

Wrenching his axe from his belt, Torak put the fire between them once more. 'How can the World Spirit be on your side? Killing hunters? How can that please the Spirit?'

'To offer a hunter to the fire is to give it the noblest death of all. It is the Way.'

Again the whip cracked, Torak dodged, and the rawhide struck stone. 'It's not the clans' way,' he panted, 'and it's not your Forest.'

'I am the Master!' boomed Thiazzi. 'I have taken the Deep Forest for my own!' Foam flew from his lips, and his green eyes glittered.

As Torak stared at him, everything fell into place. 'The war between the clans. You started it. You set them against each other.'

Yellow teeth flashed in the russet beard.

'You planted the curse sticks,' said Torak, moving backwards, nearly losing his footing. 'You murdered the Forest Horse Mage and blamed it on the Aurochs. You made them fight.'

'They wanted to fight. They *needed* to fight!'

The whip bit Torak's wrist, and with a cry he dropped his axe. He lunged for it, but Thiazzi was faster, snatching it and throwing it on the fire. 'The clans are *weak*,' he snarled. 'They've forgotten the True Way, but *I* will unite them. That's why the World Spirit gave this land to me: to root out differences, to return the clans to the Way! No more clan guardians, no more clan Mages. One way. One Forest. One Leader!'

Dashing the sweat from his eyes, Torak pulled his knife from its sheath.

Again, Thiazzi's yellow grin flashed. 'I *cannot* be hurt!' He pointed to the mistletoe at his breast. 'The deathless heart of the oak shields me from harm! I am invincible!'

Torak's knife trembled in his hand.

'But come,' taunted the Oak Mage, 'try your luck. Let's see if you can break me. Or shall I break you, as easily as I broke your mother and your father?'

The red mist descended. Torak saw him through a haze of blood.

' . . . As I broke your kinsman,' boasted the Oak Mage. 'As I threw him over the Crag and spattered his brains across the rocks . . . '

Torak roared and launched himself at Thiazzi.

Wolf stalked the not-aurochs upwind, which he would never normally do. But this time, he *wanted* them to smell him.

A cow caught his scent and swung round. Wolf lowered his head to tell her he was hunting. The cow gave a nervous snort and pawed the earth. Wolf came on. She charged. Wolf dodged her nimbly and ran off to worry a bull. The bull rounded on him. Wolf leapt clear of his horns by a whisker and bounded away. He was enjoying this.

Now the whole herd was anxious. It stopped munching willowherb and started lumbering up the slope. Wolf prowled behind a cluster of young cows who were huffing and showing the whites of their eyes. He chose the edgiest and snapped at her fetlock. The cow squealed, jerked up her tail and fled. Panicked, the rest of the herd followed.

Up the ridge they went, with Wolf racing after them, loping this way and that, so they'd think they were hunted by many hungry wolves. Rocks fell and branches snapped as they crashed into the next valley, down towards Tall Tailless and the Bitten One.

The earth shook as Wolf drove them on, and his heart leapt. *This* was what one wolf could do!

NINETEEN

A t first, Torak thought it was a rockfall.

The earth shook as if the Mountains were falling. He froze, knife in hand. The thunder swelled to a roar. A bison crashed into the grove. Torak ran for his life.

He reached the hollies, threw himself at the nearest branch, and swung himself up – as the grove was engulfed by a heaving torrent of hoof and horn.

Like a flash flood, the bison swept through, and Torak clung to the shuddering tree. The din pounded through him. It was never going to end.

It did. The silence after it had gone was deafening. A pall of smoke and dust hung in the air, with the musky smell of bison. The Great Oak and the Great Yew towered above it: inviolate, their branches pricking the night sky.

As the dust settled, Torak saw sparks from the trampled

fire scattered like stars over the ground. He dropped to earth and ran to search the grove. Thiazzi was gone.

In disbelief, Torak stumbled about in the gloom, searching the stony slopes. Nothing. The pounding hooves had obliterated all hope of a trail. Thiazzi had vanished like smoke.

'*No!*' shouted Torak. The echoes died. Pebbles fell like a rattle of stony laughter.

He slumped onto a boulder. He'd lost his chance for vengeance.

Wolf bounded out of the darkness and pounced on him joyously. His fur was full of burrs, and fluffed up with excitement. Torak had no idea why.

Much prey, Torak told Wolf wearily. *Nearly trampled. Good you weren't here.*

To Torak's bemusement, Wolf dropped his ears, gave an embarassed yawn, and rolled onto his back, saying sorry.

Torak asked him if the Bitten One was close.

Gone, was all Wolf would say.

Torak rubbed a hand over his face. He'd achieved nothing. The only thing to do now was make the long trudge back to the Red Deer camp, and try to persuade them that the Forest Horse Mage was indeed Thiazzi. And start all over again.

A great weariness swept over him. He missed Renn. She would be furious with him for leaving her; but whatever she said couldn't be as bad as what he was saying to himself.

By moonset, he'd reached the end of the valley of the horses and could go no further. He found a fallen tree a few paces above the Windriver and made it into an inadequate shelter with branches and mouldy bracken. He'd left his sleeping-sack with the Red Deer, but he was too tired to care; he would drag in more bracken for bedding. After chewing a slip of dried horse meat and tucking the last of it in a birch tree for the Forest, he wrapped his nettlestem mantle about him and fell asleep.

This time, he knows he is dreaming. He is lying on his back in the shelter, but above him the sky is a blizzard of stars. He is in a cold sweat of terror, but he cannot move. A shadow darkens the stars as something leans over him. Wet hair slithers over his face. He hears the soft creak of mouldering seal hide. His flesh shrinks from icy breath.

It's lonely at the bottom of the Sea . . . Fish eat my flesh. The Sea Mother rolls my bones. It's cold. So cold.

Torak tries to speak. His lips won't move.

Why didn't you come to me on the Crag? I was lonely, waiting for you. I'm lonelier now. And so cold . . .

Torak woke with a start.

Dawn had not yet come. He hadn't slept long. Wolf was gone, but Rip and Rek were hopping about outside the shelter, cawing. *Wake up, wake up!*

Torak dug the heels of his hands into his eyes. 'I'm sorry, kinsman. I missed my chance. But I'll find him again, I swear. I will avenge you.'

The ravens would watch over Tall Tailless, and Wolf would not go far. But he couldn't ignore those howls.

He had heard them in his sleep. Darkfur had come down from the Mountain, she was trying to find him! Then he'd woken up, and disappointment had crushed him. She was in the *other* Now, not this one.

But he'd heard her again. Very faint and far away, but it was her. He would know her howl anywhere.

Panting with eagerness, he loped through the Forest. As the Light came, he leapt a little Fast Wet, and splashed through a bigger one. Tall Tailless would be all right with the ravens. And Wolf would not be away for long.

The ravens flew from tree to tree, fluffing up their head-feathers and making stony chuk-chuk warning calls.

Warning of what? wondered Torak.

Dawn was breaking as he left the Windriver and headed north, towards the Red Deer camp. The wind was gusting, the trees moaning. His misgivings grew: a tightness in the chest that made it hard to breathe.

Others felt it too. Birds fled across the sky – jays, magpies, crows. Reindeer cantered past, scarcely swerving to avoid him, as if escaping a greater threat. Torak thought of Renn and quickened his pace.

Ahead, a figure emerged from behind a rowan, and he recognized the Red Deer woman with the bark-bound head. She dithered, then overcame her shyness and ran down to him. 'At last!' she said with a timid smile. 'We've been looking for you everywhere!'

'What's wrong?' he said brusquely. 'Is Renn all right?'

'She's safe with the others, it's you we were worried about. We didn't know where you'd gone.'

They headed up the trail, the woman lagging behind, Torak running ahead. He heard a distant growl of thunder. The first drops of rain pattered on the leaves, and he put up his hood. Something grabbed his ankle and yanked him high into the air.

The earth swung sickeningly. As the dizziness cleared, he realized that he was hanging by one leg from a young rowan tree – which, moments before, had been bent double.

You *fool*, he berated himself. A simple spring trap, and you blunder right into it!

His knife wasn't in its sheath. It lay where it had fallen in a clump of goosefoot, out of reach. Furious, he shouted at the woman to come and cut him down.

She came running up the trail. 'You're caught in a trap,' she said.

'Well, obviously!' he snapped. 'Cut me down!'

Her arms hung limp at her sides.

Were her wits completely gone? Snarling with frustration, Torak made a grab for the rope, which was drawn tight around his left ankle. He fell back with a growl. *'Cut me down!'*

'No,' said the woman.

'What?' The rope creaked. Rain pattered on the leaves.

Only it isn't rain, he realized. It's ash. Flakes of ash, swirling like dirty snow. And that glow in the sky, it's in the wrong place for dawn. Not east, but west. 'Fire,' he said. 'There's a fire in the Forest.'

'Yes,' said the woman in an altered voice.

Upside-down, Torak saw her pull off the bark which covered her head and shake out her long, ash-grey hair.

'The fire has escaped,' she said. 'It is eating the Forest. The Chosen One has set it free.'

TWENTY

Like a fish on a hook, Torak dangled from the tree, while the sky darkened to an angry orange twilight which had nothing to do with the sun. 'You can't leave me here to burn!' he cried.

'You are an unbeliever,' said the woman. 'You are for the fire.'

'Why? What have I done?' Bending double and hauling himself up the rope, he made a grab for the nearest branch. It snapped. He fell back, jarring his leg. 'What have I *done*?'

Squatting on her haunches, the woman peered at him. Her face was blistered and peeling, and in her lashless eyes he saw the cunning behind the madness. 'The Chosen One watches him,' she hissed. 'She sees him wake the fire with stone, she sees him dishonour it. She knows.'

'What do you *want*?'

She licked her cracked lips, and he saw the ash crusting the corners. 'To serve the Master, and through him to know the fire once more. The red so pure it makes all else grey . . . '

'But the Master wants to *rule* the Forest,' he panted. 'He can't want you to destroy it!'

She smiled. 'The Master says to watch the unbeliever, but the Chosen One will do more. She will give him to the fire.'

'Wait,' he said, desperate to keep her with him. 'Was it – was it the Master who made you the Chosen One?'

Her features lit up like embers. 'It was the fire,' she whispered. 'On a clear blue day, the lightning sought her from the sky. No thunder, no warning. Just that blazing brightness, brighter than the sun – and she at its very heart.' She leaned closer, and he smelt her acrid breath. 'In that moment, she sees *everything*. The bones in her flesh, the veins in the leaves, the fire that sleeps in every tree. She sees the truth. *Everything burns.*'

The roar of the fire was getting louder. Smoke was seeping through the trees. 'But you survived,' he said. 'The lightning let you live. You should let me live. Cut me down!'

She was oblivious, lost in her story. 'The fire took her for its own. It turned her hair to ash. It scorched the child from her womb. It *transformed* her . . . ' Her burning fingers stroked his cheek, and her smile was tender and merciless. 'It will transform you, too.'

He thought of Thiazzi's charred sacrifices on the tree. 'You can't leave me here to burn,' he pleaded.

'Listen to it grow!' With raised arms she saluted the fire. 'The more it eats, the greater its hunger! You are honoured. The fire will take you for its own.' Then she was gone.

'Don't leave me!' shouted Torak. 'Don't leave me,' he begged.

A shard of blazing bark struck the ground by his head. Around him the trees thrashed in the fire's searing breath. The sky had deepened to bloody amber. In the west, he saw it coming for him. He remembered what Fin-Kedinn had said. *It can leap into a tree faster than a lynx, and when it does — when it gets into the branches — then it goes where it likes. You wouldn't believe how fast . . .*

The Bright Beast came roaring through the Forest, faster than Wolf thought possible. It was eating everything: trees, hunters, prey. Where was Tall Tailless?

Wolf should never have left him. He hadn't found Darkfur and now he couldn't find his pack-brother.

Desperately, Wolf loped into the bitter breath of the Bright Beast. The panicked prey thundered past, fleeing the other way, and he dodged their trampling hooves. He splashed across a little Fast Wet. He skittered down a gully — and the Bright Beast reared above him, big as a Mountain. His pelt crisped, his eyes stung. He couldn't go any further, couldn't seek his pack-brother in its very jaws. It was eating everything, and if it caught him, it would eat him too.

Spinning round, he raced back up the gully, and the Bright Beast raced after him. It lashed out a glittering claw. Wolf leapt to avoid it. It pounced on a tree and ate it. Another sapling groaned — Wolf sped beneath it just before it crashed — and the Bright Beast's cubs flew through the air and devoured more trees.

Hot stones bit Wolf's pads, he ran as he'd never run

before, and the Bright Beast raced after him. It flew, it leapt from tree to tree, it soared over the Wet. It was eating the Forest. Nothing could escape.

Snarling with effort, Torak pulled himself upright and made another grab at the rowan. His fingers brushed bark, but couldn't grasp it. Yet again he fell back.

He had another try. This time, he caught a branch. He clung on. This had to work. If it didn't, he was finished.

Shaking his boot off his free foot, he slapped his bare sole against the rowan's trunk and half-kicked, half-hauled himself into the fork. He lay gasping, the tree digging into his belly. He was upright at last.

No time to rest. He wriggled and squirmed till he'd got into a crouch in the fork, supported on his right foot. His left leg, tethered to higher up the trunk, stuck out awkwardly.

Chunks of blazing bark thudded like fiery hail as he tugged at the noose around his ankle; but his weight had pulled it savagely tight around his boot, it wouldn't budge. Frantically he worked at the knot. His right calf trembled with the strain of supporting him.

The noose gave slightly. He worked at it. It loosened a little more. It was all he needed. Twisting and tugging, he yanked his foot from his boot, wriggled out of the noose, and jumped to earth.

After a desperate scramble in the undergrowth, he found his knife and staggered to his feet. His eyes were streaming, his skin prickling with heat. Smoke had turned day to night.

A roe buck sped past. He guessed it was heading for

wetlands and ran after it. Cinders stung his feet. He was barefoot. No time to go back for his boots.

As he ran, he glanced over his shoulder. Flames taller than trees were licking at the sky. The noise was like nothing he'd ever heard, it was the thunder of a thousand thousand bison, it seized his heart and squeezed it dry, it sucked the air from his lungs.

He dropped to a crouch and gulped cleaner air, and when he straightened up, the smoke was so thick that he couldn't see his hand in front of his face. He didn't know where he was, but he knew he had to decide now, this instant, which way to run – or he would die.

A loud cark!

He couldn't see the ravens but he heard them calling to him as they flew high above the smoke. Blindly, he followed their cries. Burning branches rained down. He was running in the very breath of the fire, and all around him trees were snapping and groaning.

Again he glanced back. A river of flame slithered up a pine tree, which exploded in a shower of sparks. A woodgrouse flew skywards, then dropped back again, sucked to its death in the burning wind.

Quork! Quork! called Rip and Rek. *Follow!*

Suddenly the ground was gone and Torak was rolling and bumping downhill.

He jolted to a halt and struggled to his knees. Hands and feet sank into mud: cold, wet, blessed mud. The ravens had led him to a lake. He splashed into the shallows – and fell headlong over a rock.

The rock gave a piteous whinny. It was a foal, a small black foal, sunk to its knobbly fetlocks in mud, shaking with terror. It was too frightened to move, but Torak couldn't stop to help. He waded past.

Ahead of him, the murk thinned for a moment, and in the lake he made out the bobbing black heads of horses swimming for their lives, and beyond them a beaver lodge as big as a Raven shelter.

Another anguished whinny from the foal – and in the lake, one of the black heads turned. The mother must have waited as long as she dared, but when her foal wouldn't follow, she'd had to leave. Now she swam reluctantly with the herd, forced to leave her young one to its doom.

That was what Torak should do: swim for the beaver lodge and leave the foal to burn.

With a growl, he turned back, grabbed a handful of its spiky mane, and pulled.

The foal rolled its white-rimmed eyes and refused to budge. 'Come on!' yelled Torak. '*Swim!* It's your last chance!' That only made things worse. The foal didn't understand people talk, but what was Torak supposed to do? If he said it in wolf talk, it'd die of fright.

Getting behind the little creature, he shoved his head under its belly and heaved it onto his shoulders. It struggled feebly, so he grabbed its legs to hold it still, and staggered into the lake.

When he was waist-deep, he chucked the foal in the water. 'You're on your own!' he shouted above the clamour of the fire. 'Swim!' He threw himself in and struck out for the beaver lodge.

The fire's name-soul glared at him from the water. Over his shoulder, he saw it claiming the slope down which he'd fallen. He saw the foal swimming bravely behind him.

He was nearly at the beaver lodge, and tiring fast. Billows of black smoke rolled towards him. He couldn't breathe. He'd intended to climb onto the lodge and shelter there till the fire had leapt the lake, but now he realized that if he did, he would choke to death. He had to get inside. Beaver lodges have a sleeping-chamber above water level, which the beavers reach by underwater tunnels. Torak took a deep breath and dived.

Groping at branches, he sought the mouth of a tunnel. His chest was bursting. He couldn't find a tunnel, couldn't see a thing, it was like swimming in mud.

He found an opening. Squeezed through it – burst from the water – and struck his head on a sapling.

He could barely see in the red gloom, but the roar of the fire wasn't quite so deafening. Through the stench of smoke, he caught the musky stink of beaver, but he couldn't see any; maybe the fire had overtaken them on the shore.

They had built their lodge well. The sleeping-platform was littered with wood chips to keep it snug and dry, while above, the branches were loosely packed to make an air vent which reached to the top of the lodge. The sleeping-platform was only beaver high, and Torak didn't want to get stuck, so he decided to stay in the water and wait out the fire.

Gasping for breath, he thanked the beavers and Rip and Rek and the Forest for his shelter.

'Please,' he panted, *'please* keep Wolf and Renn safe.'

His words were lost in the roar of the fire, and he felt in his heart that it was hopeless. The fire was eating the Forest. Nothing could survive.

Not Wolf. Not Renn.

TWENTY-ONE

Renn stumbled about in a world burnt black.

The Forest was gone. It simply wasn't there any more. She wandered between charcoal spikes which had once been trees. She felt their bewildered souls thronging the soot-laden air, but was too devastated to pity them. Even the sun was gone, swallowed up in an unearthly grey half-light. Had the fire taken the whole Forest? The Open Forest as well as the Deep?

The stink made her cough, and the sound echoed eerily. When she stopped, all she could hear was a furtive crackle of embers, the occasional crash of a falling tree.

Death, she thought, death everywhere. Where is Torak? Is he alive? Or is he . . .

No. Don't think it. He's with Wolf. They are both alive, and so is Fin-Kedinn, and Rip and Rek.

Rubbing her face, she felt the grittiness of soot. She was covered in it. She tasted it on her tongue. Her eyes were swollen and sore. She'd swallowed so much smoke she felt sick.

She was thirsty, too, but she had no waterskin. Only her axe and knife and the wovenstem quiver the Red Deer had given her, containing her last three arrows. And of course her bow.

To give herself courage, she unslung it from her shoulder and rubbed the grime from its waist. Golden heartwood gleamed, and she thought of Fin-Kedinn making it for her many summers ago, and felt a little less alone.

But her thirst was becoming pressing, and it was a long time since she'd left the lake. She had no idea which way she'd come. Where *was* she?

She should never have escaped from the Red Deer.

Durrain had sensed the fire almost before the prey, and the whole clan had taken to the lake, seeking refuge in canoes which they'd moored to the islet in the middle. There Renn had done as they did, soaking her cloak, huddling beneath it.

She hadn't been frightened, not then. She'd been too angry with Torak for leaving her. A whole day of patient questioning. *Where did he go? I don't know. Where did he go?* It astonished her that they didn't guess, but they seemed to think it impossible that anyone would brave the sacred grove alone. It would've served him right, she'd thought furiously, if she *had* given him away.

But as she lay in the rocking gloom with the fire roaring towards them, she forgot her anger. A child sobbed. A woman whispered a charm. Renn shut her eyes and prayed for Torak and Wolf. Please, please, let them live.

Then it burst upon them, and the canoe rocked wildly and people shouted prayers.

It had taken Renn a while to realize that the fire had jumped the lake and swept on without devouring them. Then the World Spirit had lanced the clouds and released a torrent of rain, and in the confusion, she'd slipped overboard and swum away.

She *thought* she'd headed south, but in the smoke and the rain it was hard to tell. Now, as a breeze cleared the haze, she saw that she stood in a narrow gully where a stream had once run. Maybe it led to a river.

She hadn't gone far when a branch crashed behind her. She turned. The dead trees looked like hunters stalking her.

One of them moved.

She ran, blundering down the gully. She ran till she had to stop, hands on knees, gasping for breath.

Around her, the gully was quiet. Whatever had moved, hadn't come after her. Maybe it had been a tree, after all.

She stumbled between the smoking spikes. Beyond a spur, she saw green. She blinked. Yes, *green*!

Moaning, she rounded the spur – and the green of the Forest blinded her. Rowan and beech and whitebeam rose before her, their boughs a little sooty, but alive.

Panting with relief, she sank to her knees amid ferns and celandine. By her hand lay a sky-blue shard of thrush's egg, pushed from the nest by the hatchling. On a log she saw a spruce sapling as tall as her thumb, thrusting bravely through the moss. She thought, the Forest is eternal. Nothing can conquer it.

But there was no sign of a river. Straining for sounds of water, she wandered through the trees.

At last she was halted by a grove of tall pines which had

been toppled by a storm. Dead trunks and earthy root discs blocked her way in a criss-crossed tangle. She ought to turn back, that was what you did when you were lost. But she couldn't face returning to the wasteland.

The pines didn't want her in their bone-ground. Their mossy trunks tried to throw her off, their branches jutted like spears. It was a relief to get out the other side, back among living oaks and limes.

But these trees didn't want her, either. Furrowed bark faces glared at her, and twig fingers dragged at her hair. Some of the trunks were hollow. She thought what it would be like to be trapped inside, and hurried on.

The wind strengthened, blowing soot in her face. She coughed and went on coughing, doubled up, leaning against a tree.

Beneath her fingers, she felt eyes.

With a cry she snatched her hand away.

Yes, eyes. A fierce red gaze had been carved in the trunk, and a square mouth, edged with real human teeth.

Renn had never seen such a thing. She guessed it had been done to give voice to the tree's spirit. But who would give a tree teeth?

Uneasily, she scanned her surroundings. Lime trees, nettles, a scattering of boulders.

She went on.

When she glanced back, the trees had moved. They'd been much closer to that boulder, she was sure of it. Now they were more spread out.

She started to run.

A root tripped her and she fell – and came face to face with another trunk mask, its eyes tight shut in its lichen-crusted face.

Panting, she got to her feet.

The eyes opened. Bark limbs detached themselves from the trunk. Bark hands reached to grab her.

Whimpering, she fled.

To her left, another bark creature separated from a trunk. Then another and another. Bark people moved to surround her, reaching for her with ridged hands and blank, fissured faces.

As she ran, her axe banged against her thigh. She wrenched it from her belt, but knew that she'd never dare use it.

Her breath rasped in her throat. With nightmare slowness she waded through piles of crackling leaves. She stumbled down a slope and into another tree bone-ground where she wobbled over fallen trunks, while the bark people ran along them like fire, hunting her in eerie silence.

Something yanked at her shoulder, pulling her back. Her bow had snagged on a branch. She struggled to free it.

Bark hands seized her and dragged her down.

TWENTY-TWO

'W here are you taking me?' said Renn.

The bark men did not reply.

'Please. Why won't you speak? What have I done?'

One of them jabbed at her with his spear. She didn't wait for him to do it again.

All day she had walked in a silent throng of hunters. They'd taken her weapons, but they hadn't touched her again. They seemed to regard her as unclean.

In vain she'd begged them for water. They ignored her. She stumbled through a haze of thirst and a forest of poisoned spears.

She had no idea where she was. The great fire hadn't touched this part of the Forest, but its stench hung in the air, so she guessed that the wasteland wasn't far.

From her captors' green headbands and horn amulets,

she guessed they were Aurochs, but in her mind they were the bark people. Their clothes were yellowish-brown wovenbark, and rolls of bark pierced their earlobes. Their shaven scalps were caked with yellow clay to resemble bark, and the men's beards were clogged with it, like straggly tree-roots. But unlike the Aurochs she'd seen at clan meets, they hadn't stopped there. They had carved their very flesh into bark, disfiguring their hands and faces with rough, ridged scars.

Renn knew a little about such scars. Some of her own clan, including Fin-Kedinn, bore a raised zigzag on each arm, to ward off demons. Creating them was very painful. After slitting the skin with a sliver of flint, a paste of ash and lichen was rubbed in, and the wound bound tight. Renn thought about having her face slashed, and felt sick.

They reached another stream, and again she begged to be allowed to drink. The hunters stared at her, their eyes unresponsive. *No drink.*

The light was failing when they finally reached camp. By then she was dizzy with thirst.

The Auroch camp lay in a hollow guarded by watchful spruce. Smouldering pine knots dispersed a smoky orange light and an eye-stinging tang of tree-blood. Birch-bark shelters squatted round a central pine. Outside each shelter lay a pile of wooden shields like a nest of giant beetles, and a fire ringed with stones. From the trunk of the pine hung an auroch's horned skull.

Beneath it, a group of silent children twisted piles of pounded spruce root into twine. All stared at Renn without expression. Like the adults, their faces were disfigured with ridges, many still crusted with blood.

Renn couldn't see anyone who looked like a Leader or a Mage, but she noticed that not everyone was Auroch.

There was another clan here, too. Dark hair was braided tight, two braids for women, one for men, and faces were unscarred, but dusted red with ground pine bast. In fact, everything was stained red: lips, partings, even fingernails. The women were dressed in plain buckskin, but the men wore splendid belts of black and gold fur. Lynx Clan.

Auroch or Lynx, all gave her the same unfeeling stare. They didn't know what pity was.

As her captors approached the fires, they squatted in the smoke, wafting it over themselves. They pushed Renn in too, as if to cleanse her, then dragged her to the pine tree and forced her to her knees.

Women emerged from the shelters. Like the men, their faces were bark-scarred, but their caked scalps were studded with tiny alder cones, and they wore tunics, not leggings.

One carried a waterskin.

'Please,' mumbled Renn. 'I'm so thirsty.'

The woman glared at her.

Weakly, Renn beat the ground with her fists. 'Please!'

An old man stooped and peered at her. He was the ugliest, hairiest old man she'd ever seen. Although he was Auroch, he hadn't shaved his scalp, but had simply smeared his mane and beard with clay, which hung in clots. Bristles sprouted from his ears and nostrils, and his brows were tangled creepers overhanging the caverns of his eyes.

With a horny finger he prodded her greenstone wrist-guard.

She jerked back.

He spat in disgust and hobbled away.

A younger man emerged from a shelter. His face was a web of scars.

Renn pointed to the waterskin. 'Please,' she begged.

Using hand speech, the man gave a command, and the woman set the waterskin before Renn.

She fell on it and drank greedily. Almost at once, the throbbing in her head eased, and strength flooded back into her limbs. '*Thank* you,' she said.

Another woman brought a large bark bowl which she placed before the hunters. Renn felt a surge of hope. The food smelt good. It made the Aurochs seem a little more human.

The woman scooped some into a smaller bowl and put it in a fork of the pine as an offering. Then she scooped up another helping and laid it before Renn.

It was an appetising stew of nettles and scraps of meat, possibly squirrel, and Renn's belly growled.

The woman bunched her fingers to her mouth and nodded. *Eat.*

The man who'd allowed her to drink cleared his throat. 'You,' he said to Renn in a voice which sounded hoarse from disuse. 'You must rest. And eat.'

Renn looked from him to the bowl, then back again.

They told me to rest, Gaup had said. *They gave me food. Then they cut off my hand.*

TWENTY-THREE

Fear is the loneliest feeling. You can be in a throng of people, but if you're afraid, you're on your own.

Renn felt like an offering being prepared for sacrifice. When she refused to eat, she was taken to a pool and made to wash, while women wiped the soot from her clothes with moss. By hiding in the reeds, she managed to conceal the beaver-tooth knife tied to her calf and the grouse-bone whistle at her neck; but when they gave her back her clothes, her clan-creature feathers were gone.

Back at camp, hunger got the better of her and she forced down some of the stew under the watchful gaze of both clans. Scarred hands flickered in silent speech, and a young man with a mouth like a sliver of flint sharpened an axe and eyed her wrists.

The hairy old man sat cross-legged, straightening a pile

of arrowshafts. Renn watched him drawing each stick through a grooved piece of antler. Her own clan used the same method. Now and then, he slapped one hairy paw with a bunch of nettles to sting away the stiffening sickness. Older Ravens did that, too.

She edged closer to him. 'What will they do to me?' she said in a low voice.

He scowled and bent over his arrows.

She asked if he was the Clan Leader.

He shook his head and pointed an arrowshaft at the man who'd ordered that she be given water.

'Are you the Mage?'

Another shake of the head. 'I make the best bows in the Deep Forest,' he growled.

'Don't talk to her,' warned the young man with the axe. He clapped his hand to his mouth. 'She tricked me into talking! She's a Forest Horse spy!'

'I've never even met a Forest Horse,' protested Renn.

'We *hate* them,' muttered the young man.

'But why?' she said. 'You all follow the Way.'

'We follow it better,' he snapped. 'They use a bow to waken fire. We use sticks. That's proof.'

'Only *we* follow the *True* Way,' said a clay-headed woman. 'That's why we bear the scars. To punish ourselves for ever having left it.'

'All other clans are wicked,' declared the young man, sprinkling sand on his grindstone.

Renn thought that if she could keep them talking, maybe they wouldn't hurt her. She asked him why.

He glared at her. 'The Mountain clans are wicked because they use stone to waken fire, and worship the fire spirit. There *is* no fire spirit, there is only tree! Ice and Sea clans are wicked because they live in terrible lands that *have* no trees, and wake false fire from the fat of fishes. You in the Open Forest are worst, because you *knew* the Way, but turned your backs on it.'

An Auroch woman threw him a reproving glance. 'Don't talk to her, she's evil. She stole my child!'

'No I didn't,' said Renn.

'No more talk!' ordered the Auroch Clan Leader.

After that, they made her crouch among the roots of the pine tree. Men scowled at her. A girl spat in her face. Her hand went to her grouse-bone whistle, but she saw the young man staring, and tucked it back in her jerkin.

The camp had fallen silent again, but hands flickered, weaving hidden meanings. Renn thought of the Raven camp, with its squabbling children and dogs nosing for scraps, and Fin-Kedinn telling stories by the fire. Her heart twisted with longing. Fin-Kedinn, help me. What do I do?

Clear and bright, she remembered a frosty morning many winters ago, when he'd taken her into the Forest to try out her new bow. She hadn't wanted to go. Her fa had just died, and the other children were ganging up on her; she'd wanted to stay in her sleeping-sack and never come out. But there was her uncle, warming his hands at the fire, waiting for her.

Their breath had smoked as they'd crunched through the snow. Fin-Kedinn had found tracks and shown her how to read them. 'When the red deer know that the wolves are hunting them, they trot proudly and lift their hooves high. *See how strong I am*, they're telling the wolves. *Don't attack me, I can fight back!*' His blue eyes met hers. He wasn't only talking about the deer.

Renn gripped the pine roots with both hands. Fin-Kedinn was right. She would not sit meekly while others decided her fate. 'What are you saying about me?' she called in a voice which carried across the camp.

Heads turned. Hands stilled.

'If you're deciding what to do with me, tell me. Keeping it from me – that's not justice.'

The Auroch Leader stood up. 'The Aurochs are always just.'

'Then talk to me,' said Renn.

For the first time, the Lynx Leader spoke. 'Who *are* you?'

She rose to her feet. 'I am Renn of the Raven Clan. I am a Mage.' As soon as she said it, she knew it was true.

'Women can't be Mages,' sneered the young man with the axe. 'It's against the Way. I'll show you how much of a Mage she is!' He ran to snatch her grouse-bone whistle.

'Stay away!' she warned. 'This is a Mage's bone for summoning spirits! None may touch it but me!'

He drew back as if she'd burnt him.

Putting the whistle to her lips, she blew. 'None of you can hear its voice,' she said, 'but I can. This bone speaks only to Mages and to spirits.'

Now she had the whole camp's attention. Raising her head, she cawed a raven summons to the stars. Then she held up her hands and showed the zigzag tattoos on her inner wrists. 'See the marks I bear! It's lightning: the spears of the World Spirit, who chases demons into rocks and wakes the fire from trees. Harm shall come to any who attempts to harm me!'

That was an eerie echo of her mother, but she didn't care; whatever else she was, Seshru had been a powerful Mage.

Above the trees, she saw the gibbous moon riding high. It had been dead when Bale was killed, but now it was stronger. So was she.

'If she's a Mage,' said the Lynx Leader, 'she's an Open Forest Mage. The World Spirit doesn't want her here. That's why it stays away.'

A nodding of heads and fluttering of hands.

'She stole my child,' repeated the Auroch woman. 'She took him for a tokoroth!'

'No,' said Renn. 'I hunt the one who did.'

'And who is that?' said the Auroch Leader suspiciously.

'Thiazzi,' she replied. 'Thiazzi the Oak Mage.'

People frowned in disbelief, and the old man looked disappointed, as if he'd caught Renn lying. 'There's no-one left from the Oak Clan,' he said. 'They all died out.'

'The Soul-Eater didn't,' said Renn. 'Take me to your Mage and I'll give him proof.'

'Our Mage keeps to his prayer shelter,' said the Auroch Leader, 'he doesn't see outsiders.'

'If you were really a Mage,' snarled the young man, 'you'd know that.'

People nodded. The throng closed in around her. Scarred faces leered. Red hands gripped poisoned spears. Her knees shook, but she stood her ground. To waver now was to fall.

A harsh caw echoed through the Forest.

All heads turned skywards.

A shadow cut across the stars – and Rip lit onto a pine branch, his black eyes fixed on Renn.

She cawed a greeting and he swooped, landing with a thud on her shoulder. Talons dug into her parka, stiff feathers brushed her cheek. She made a gurgling sound, and Rip raised his bill and half-spread his wings in reply.

People drew back, clutching clan-creature amulets.

At the edge of camp, a wolf appeared.

Relief washed over Renn. If Wolf had survived the fire, maybe Torak had too.

Wolf's amber eyes grazed the camp, then returned to Renn. His hackles bristled. The sinews of his long legs were taut. One sign from her and he would spring to her aid.

He had helped her simply by showing himself. It would be dangerous for him to do more. 'Uff,' she warned.

He tilted his head, puzzled.

'Uff!' she said again.

He turned and vanished into the trees.

The clans breathed out. The young man stood dumbstruck, his axe dangling from his hand.

The old man cleared his throat. 'I think,' he said, 'we'd better not harm her just yet.'

Wolf was frightened and confused. His paws hurt from the hot earth, and he couldn't find Tall Tailless because the Bright Beast had eaten all the scents. And now the pack-sister had howled to him, then told him to go.

He didn't. He stayed near the Den.

The taillesses stank of fear and hatred. They hated the pack-sister, but were too scared to hurt her. The pack-sister was frightened too, but she hid it extremely well. This was something taillesses did much better than normal wolves.

Not far from the Den, Wolf found a small Still Wet, and cooled his sore pads in the mud. He waded deeper and washed the stink of the Bright Beast off his fur.

When he got back to the Den, he scented a change. The

151

taillesses were getting ready to move. Wolf decided to follow and keep a close nose on the pack-sister.

Then maybe Tall Tailless would come too.

Two Lynx hunters ran into camp, breathless and sweating, and spoke to the Leaders in a flurry of hand speech. Renn tried and failed to follow what was going on.

Wolf had gone, but the ravens were playing in the pine tree, hanging by their talons from the auroch horns, then dropping almost to the ground before soaring and swooping round for another turn.

The young man cast them hostile looks, but the old man shrugged. 'They're ravens, they like games. And trickery.'

Renn wondered if that was meant for her.

'Here,' he said, 'you might as well take this, although I can't let you have any arrows.'

To her astonishment, he held out her bow. It had been cleaned and oiled, the bowstring freshly waxed.

'Thank you,' she said.

He grunted. 'It's a good bow, and you've looked after it. Unlike some.' He shuddered in sympathy for all mistreated bows. 'But the string's frayed. Give me your spare and I'll replace it.'

Renn hesitated. 'This *is* the spare string,' she lied.

He peered at her through the tangle of his brows.

Had he laid a trap for her? Or was he telling her to use what she had? She was about to ask why he'd given it back when the young man ran over to them.

'It's decided,' he told the old man, 'We're breaking camp.'

'Where to?' said Renn.

He ignored her, but the old one gave her a regretful

look. 'I'm sorry,' he muttered as he hobbled away.

Renn barely had time to sling her bow over her shoulder before her wrists were tied and a blindfold was pulled over her eyes.

TWENTY-FOUR

After the darkness of the beaver lodge, daylight blinded Torak.

Blinking, spitting out lake water, he clung to a branch. It was sooty; his hand came away black. The air was hazed with bitter brown smoke.

Scrambling onto the piled branches of the lodge, he cast about. Dimly, he made out charcoal hills jagged with dead trees. Nothing else.

He sank to his knees. Renn. Wolf. How could they have survived?

If there had been a single bird in the sky, he would have broken his promise to the wind and spirit walked to find them. If there had been a single tree left alive on the slopes . . .

Behind him, something sneezed.

The foal lay in a sprawl of spindly legs. It looked as startled as Torak by its sneeze.

Gently, he stroked its mane, and it blinked at him through long lashes. He felt a spark of hope. If a foal could live through the fire, maybe Wolf and Renn had too.

Talking to the foal in an undertone, he untied his belt and looped it over its neck. It wobbled to its feet and swayed. Then it threw down its head and coughed.

After a short struggle, he got it into the water, and together they struck out for the shore.

They'd hardly made it to the shallows when a shrill whinny rang out. The foal gave an answering whinny, startlingly loud, and tugged at the rawhide. Torak released it and it wobbled towards a black shape moving among the trees. Mother and foal nuzzled each other, then the foal ducked under her belly to suckle.

Torak made out more horses. The lead mare turned and gave him a penetrating stare – and in that moment, he knew what to do.

Feverishly, he took the last of Saeunn's root from his medicine pouch and crammed it in his mouth. If Wolf or Renn were anywhere in this devastation, who better to sense them than prey?

The other horses side-stepped and tossed their heads, uneasy at his nearness, but the lead mare stood her ground. Swivelling her ears, she listened to his moans as the cramps took hold. She lowered her head and watched him clutch his belly, falling to the ground in a cloud of ash . . .

. . . and through her horse eyes, Torak stared at the body which lay twitching and frothing at the mouth.

For the first time in his life, he felt the ceaseless vigilance of prey. He twisted one ear to listen to the human kicking at cinders, and flicked back the other to catch the nicker of a mare chivvying her foal. One eye scanned the shore for hunters, the other the slope above, while his horse nose told him the movements of every member of the herd.

The mare's souls were surprisingly strong, but very fearful, and although Torak wanted her to canter up the hill, she refused. She was a wise horse, she knew it was best to avoid anything strange, and since *everything* was strange, she wouldn't budge. Her herd had been through the terrors of the fire, and now they found themselves in this black Forest where there was no grazing and only the water smelt the same, so she would stay near that.

But the alien souls in her marrow were making her restive. She snorted and rolled her eyes, and the worried herd did the same.

In the battle of souls, Torak overcame her. Kicking up his hind hooves, he broke into a canter. With effortless strength his four legs hammered the earth. Such power, such speed! He felt a surge of wild joy as he thundered up the hill, and his herd came thundering after him.

At the top he halted, puffing and blowing. The ashen wind played in his mane, cooling his sweaty neck. He flared his nostrils to catch the scents.

Almost at once, he caught the scent of a wolf.

The mare shivered, remembering sharp fangs biting her flanks. Torak forced her to stay where she was. Then he heard it: a long, wavering howl. *I am seeking you . . .*

It wasn't Wolf.

The disappointment was so great that he lost control of the mare's spirit, and she wheeled and crashed down the slope. Blundering through the bemused herd, she raced back to the safety of the water.

She skittered to a halt in a cloud of ash. She smelt the

meaty breath of humans. She smelt that some bore the skins of bats, others the tails of horses. She was startled, but not frightened. Of all the hunters in the Forest, people never threatened her.

It was Torak who was afraid. He saw his human body lying defenceless on the ground. The hunters saw it too.

He saw them crunch towards him over the brittle earth, their tattooed faces merciless. He saw a Forest Horse hunter prod his body with the butt of his spear. Another kicked him in the ribs. Dimly, he felt the kick.

Now they were crowding round him, kicking, beating. With a jolt, he was back in his body, and pain was opening inside him. He moaned. Something struck his head.

In his last glimmer of awareness, he sent a silent howl to Wolf. Sorry, pack-brother, sorry I couldn't find you.

Sorry, Renn.

TWENTY-FIVE

Renn was jostled and dragged till she lost track of time. Sometimes they carried her, sometimes they tossed her in a dugout. Once they fed her food and water.

She smelt charred corpses, and knew they'd entered the wasteland. It seemed endless, but at last they were back among hooting owls and rustling leaves.

Suddenly, her wrists were untied, the blindfold torn off, and she stood blinking in a glare of firelight.

It was night. She saw torches staked in a vast ring. She caught the tang of pine, the murmur of a river. The Aurochs and Lynx had pitched their camp to one side of the ring of fire. At its centre rose a scarlet tree. Root, trunk, branch, leaf – all had been painted red with earthblood. An entire living tree was being offered, to draw the World Spirit into the Deep Forest.

Someone pushed her forwards, and she found herself beside a sputtering torch. To her amazement, she saw not only Auroch and Lynx gathered here. On the other side of the ring of fire, there was a *second* camp and a shadowy throng, bristling with axes and spears. One of them moved closer to the light, and she saw that his beard and lips were stained green, his face tattooed with leaves. His long green hair was braided with horsetails, and his headband was brown. Renn couldn't believe it. The Forest Horse Clan was camped not an arrowshot away from their deadly enemies.

Among the Forest Horses, others flitted, half-seen in the moonlight. Their mantles were the colour of night; a web of charcoal lines obscured their faces. Renn saw thorny black tattooes on their chins. Bat Clan.

The two sides faced each other across twenty paces of smoky torchlight. Arrows were nocked to bows. Hands flexed on axes and spears.

At the roots of the scarlet tree, Renn made out a huge figure in flowing robes and a glaring mask crested with horsetails. Her skin crawled. Thiazzi.

His long sleeve hid his mutilated hand, but in the other he held a heavy staff incised with burnt spirals. 'See what I bear,' he told the clans in the sonorous tones Renn had last heard in the Far North. 'I, the Forest Horse Mage, bear the speaking-staff of the Auroch Clan.'

The Aurochs stirred in alarm.

'The Auroch Mage,' Thiazzi went on, 'is known for being wise and just. I have talked with him in his prayer shelter. In token of trust, he has given me his staff.'

Doubtful head-shaking among the Aurochs. What trickery was this?

As the Forest Horse Mage approached the Auroch

Leader, they aimed a thicket of spears at his chest. Thiazzi never flinched. 'To honour that trust, I return the staff to his clan.' With a bow, he proferred it to the Leader.

Even Renn had to acknowledge his bravery. If things went wrong, he would fall transfixed by twenty spears.

With a wary bow, the Auroch Leader took the staff, and Thiazzi stepped back. Slowly, the Aurochs lowered their spears.

Renn watched him return to the scarlet tree, where he addressed both sides.

'For a moon,' he told them, 'I have fasted in the sacred grove, and the Auroch Mage has fasted in his prayer shelter. To both of us the same vision has been sent.' He raised his arms. 'We must fight *no longer*! Auroch. Forest Horse. Lynx. Bat. Red Deer. We must *unite*!'

Gasps of amazement. Hands fluttered in urgent speech.

What is he after? wondered Renn. She could understand why a Soul-Eater might wish for strife, but why . . .

'We must unite,' repeated the Mage, 'against a *greater foe*!'

In the hush that followed, one could have heard the wingbeats of a moth. All eyes were on the masked Mage prowling the scarlet tree.

'Many winters ago,' he began, 'the clans turned their backs on the True Way.'

People hung their heads. Some of the Aurochs scratched their faces to reopen their wounds.

'They were punished,' said the Mage. 'Whole clans died out. Roe Deer. Beaver. Oak. Since then, more evils have assailed the people of the Deep Forest. *All* have been caused by outsiders – by unbelievers who spurn the Way.'

That's not right, thought Renn.

'Three winters ago,' said Thiazzi, his voice swelling like the wind in the pines, 'an Open Forest trickster duped the

Red Deer into sheltering him, then repaid them by creating the demon bear.'

People hissed and shook their fists.

'Two summers ago, the people of the Open Forest sent the sickness and the tokoroths . . . '

No we didn't, thought Renn, it was the Soul-Eaters!

' . . . only our vigilance kept them from the True Forest.'

Axes were shaken in triumph, spears beaten on shields. Rapt, painted faces drank it in.

'The winter before last, the Ice clans sent hordes of demons to invade us. Last spring, the Otters tried to drown us in a flood.'

This is all lies! Renn shouted in her head.

'This spring, outsiders stole our children and sent the great fire to destroy us. They failed!'

The shield-rattling intensified.

'Until now, we have only *resisted*! But now . . . ' He swept round the ring of torches, 'Now we must *fight*! *All* evils come from outsiders! They seek to destroy us because we follow the Way, but we of the Deep Forest – the *True* Forest – we shall unite! We shall rise and crush the Open Forest!'

The roar that burst from every throat shook the pines and hammered the stars.

'Cast off your headbands!' bellowed the Mage. 'Embrace your Deep Forest brothers and unite against the outsiders!'

In a frenzy, headbands were torn from brows. Auroch ran to embrace Bat, Forest Horse touched foreheads with Lynx. Beneath the scarlet tree, the Mage watched from behind his painted mask.

Suddenly, he raised both arms for silence.

People shrank back behind the torches.

'Never forget,' said Thiazzi in a voice of subtle menace, 'that the malice of outsiders is sleepless.' He paused. 'I bring proof. I bring you the very menace itself: the Open Forest spy who sought to destroy us by releasing the great fire.'

Three men bore a bundle into the ring and threw it at the feet of the Mage.

Renn made out a struggling figure entangled in a net. She bit back a cry.

The figure groaned.

It was Torak.

TWENTY-SIX

The net was wrenched open, and Torak staggered to his feet. He stood with legs braced, hands tied behind his back. Renn saw blood on his face and bruises on his chest. She saw how he swayed.

Raising his head, he looked straight at her. His eyes widened.

She mouthed his name, but he frowned. *Stay out of this.*

'On your knees.' A Forest Horse woman put her spear to his back and forced him down. She had a mistrustful face tattooed with holly leaves, and green lips tight with anger. A horse's tail cascaded over her hair, and Renn guessed she was the Leader. She bowed low to her Mage.

Thiazzi accepted the homage in silence, but Renn caught the glint of eyes behind his mask, and thought, he's enjoying this.

'Mage,' said the Leader. 'Here is the evil one who tried to destroy the True Forest. I've seen him before. Two summers ago, we caught him trying to poison us with the sickness.'

'I was seeking the cure,' said Torak. He sounded spent.

'We should have hung him then,' said the Leader. 'We should make good the mistake.'

People rattled spears on shields in violent assent.

Renn threw herself forward, but two hairy paws held her back. 'Stay silent,' the old Auroch man hissed in her ear. 'You'll only make it worse.'

Releasing her, he took the speaking-staff from his Leader and shambled forwards. 'But if we kill him,' he said, 'we break clan law. *Our* Mage, the Auroch Mage, wouldn't sanction this.'

'To kill an unbeliever is to do good.' Thiazzi's powerful voice filled the clearing. 'And this is no ordinary unbeliever. See the scar on his chest where he tried to conceal his evil nature. See the tattoo on his brow. The mark of the outcast.'

This was too much for Renn. 'He isn't outcast any more!' she cried. 'Fin-Kedinn took him back, all the clans agreed!'

'The Deep Forest never agreed,' replied the painted mask. 'The Raven Leader sought to change clan law. Clan law cannot be changed.'

'Except by you,' said Torak.

'Be silent!' hissed the Forest Horse Leader.

Torak raised his head and glared at Thiazzi. 'You break clan law whenever you want. Don't you, Thiazzi?'

Puzzled faces turned to the Mage.

'Slaughtering hunters,' Torak went on. 'Murdering my father. My bone kin . . . '

'Silence!' shrilled the Forest Horse Leader. 'How dare

you insult our Mage!'

'He's not your Mage,' Torak flung back as he struggled to his feet. 'He's a Soul-Eater.'

Howls of outrage from the crowd, but Thiazzi was triumphant. 'By his own mouth he condemns himself! Here's proof of his wickedness!'

'What's *wrong* with you all?' thundered Torak.

Trees stirred. Torches flickered. Even the Forest Horse Leader stepped back.

With his scarred chest and glittering eyes, Torak looked terrifying — and exactly what Thiazzi had said he was. 'Have you forgotten how to *think*?' he bellowed at the crowd. 'Doesn't it seem odd that your new Mage has suddenly grown so war-like? Can't you *see* that he's not one of you?'

Renn had never seen him so angry. His rage was like the freezing white fury of the ice bear, and it frightened her. It frightened the others, too.

Thiazzi's laugh broke the spell. 'See how desperate he is! He knows he is condemned!'

Relief shuddered through the crowd. The Mage had restored their certainty.

'I've heard enough for judgement,' declared Thiazzi. 'An outcast in the True Forest is an insult to the World Spirit. This is why the Spirit stays away. The outcast must die.'

The wind got up. The red tree sighed.

Renn stood aghast.

Torak stared stonily at Thiazzi.

'Although,' said the old man, still holding the staff, 'if this truce is to stand, the Auroch Mage must also agree.'

That brought his clan to their senses, and they watched to see how the Forest Horse Mage would respond.

Torchlight played on the wooden face. Behind it, Renn

sensed the racing thoughts. He wanted Torak dead, and soon. But if he snubbed the Aurochs, he risked a riot and the ruin of his plans.

'Of course he must agree,' Thiazzi said between his teeth. 'Tonight, the Auroch Mage keeps to his prayer shelter, as I shall keep to the sacred grove. Each clan shall paint a tree with earthblood. When both Mages return, and if we are of one mind, the outcast shall die.'

Torak woke to a raging thirst.

Horsehair ropes constricted his wrists and ankles. His bruises throbbed, his head ached. Drifting in and out of wakefulness, he tried to work out where he was. A cramped shelter. Roots against his cheek . . .

He jolted awake. They had laid him beneath the scarlet tree. Soon they would hang him from it.

He couldn't see how he was going to get out of this. How long did it take to paint a tree red? That was how long he had.

He thought of Renn. She didn't look as if she'd been beaten, so maybe they would let her live. If only she didn't try to help him.

And Wolf? He saw Wolf – if he was still alive – seeking him through the charred Forest. Lost, bewildered, howling for his pack-brother. Never getting an answer.

Helpless, Torak slid into a blazing sea of thirst.

Someone was holding his head, pouring water into his mouth.

He coughed and spluttered. His tongue was swollen, he couldn't swallow. 'Don't stop,' he pleaded. It came out a meaningless mumble.

Birch bark was rough against his lips, and a cool hand supported the back of his head. Water coursed down his throat, soaking into his flesh like a flood drenching sun-cracked earth.

'How do you feel?' whispered Renn.

'Better,' he croaked. It wasn't true, but it would be soon. Shutting his eyes, he felt strength stealing into his limbs, while Renn sawed the ropes at his wrists with her beaver-tooth knife. 'Wolf,' he muttered.

'I saw him yesterday. He's fine.'

'Thank the *Spirit*. What about –'

'The ravens are fine, too. Try to sit up, we've got to be quick.'

'How did you manage this?' he asked as she started on his ankles.

'I didn't,' she said tersely. 'Everyone's asleep, I don't know why. It's as if they've taken a sleeping-potion. It can't last much longer.'

Biting down on the pain, Torak rubbed the feeling back into his wrists, while Renn washed the blood off his face and told him how Thiazzi had declared a truce among the clans. 'He must've tricked the Auroch Mage, and now he's got them all in his power.' She paused. 'Torak, this is much bigger than we thought. He's turning them against the Open Forest.'

He was trying to take that in when they heard a noise outside. A sleepy murmur, horrifyingly close. A rustle of wovenbark that subsided in a snore.

When all was quiet again, Torak breathed out. 'Why didn't they tie you up too?'

Renn strapped her knife to her calf and yanked her legging over it. 'They're scared of me . . . Because I'm a Mage.'

He met her eyes in the red darkness. Her face was sternly beautiful, and a shiver ran down his spine.

Then she was his friend again, reaching behind her and thrusting a pair of buckskin boots at him. 'I stole them from a Lynx. They'd better fit.'

As he pulled them on, she peered from the shelter. 'Can you walk?'

'I'll have to.'

The moon had set and the torches had burned out; both camps were dark and still. Around the shelter, four hunters sprawled asleep beside their weapons. Their breathing was so faint that at first Torak thought they were dead. He grabbed a bow and a quiver, jammed an axe in his belt.

Crossing the open ground to the torches seemed to take for ever. His head throbbed. Pain flared in his bruised limbs at every step. Renn vanished into the shadows, and he thought he'd lost her. She reappeared with her bow and a quiver, and pressed something into his hands. It was his knife.

'How did you – '

'I told you, they're all asleep!'

At last they were past the Auroch camp, huddled behind a clump of junipers. Renn leaned close, her hair tickling his cheek. 'They brought me here blindfold, I don't know where we are. Do you?'

He nodded. 'We came in dugouts. The Blackwater's about twenty paces over there. We'll take a boat and head upriver. Then we leave the boat and cross into the next valley, that's the valley of the horses. From there it's straight to the sacred grove.'

She frowned. 'Let's get to the boats.'

They reached the river without mishap, and found a line of dugouts drawn up on the bank. Quietly, they pushed the end boat into the shallows, and Torak climbed in. The pain of his bruises was gone, numbed by the thrill of the chase. 'The current's not strong,' he said softly. 'If we paddle hard, we might even overtake him.'

Renn stood in the shallows with her boots strung around her neck, but made no move to get in. 'Torak. Turn the boat around.'

'What?' he said impatiently.

'We can't go after Thiazzi. Not now.'

He stared at her.

'If you killed him now,' she whispered, 'you'd be confirming every lie he's told them about the Open Forest.'

'But – Renn. What are you saying?'

'We have to go back to the Open Forest. Find Fin-Kedinn. Warn the clans what's happening.'

'You can't mean this.'

Wading closer, she gripped the dugout with both hands. 'Torak, I've *seen* these people! They do everything he says. Slashing their faces, cutting off hands. They will attack the Open Forest!'

He began to be angry. 'I swore an oath, Renn. I swore to avenge my kinsman.'

'This is bigger than vengeance. Can't you see? If Thiazzi dies, they'll think it's an Open Forest plot.'

'But he's not their Mage! Once he's dead, they'll see that!'

'They won't *care*! Torak, *think*! If you killed him, they'd see it as proof of what he said. They'd attack. The Open Forest would fight back. There'd be no stopping it!'

He wanted to grab her by the shoulders and shake her. 'You said you'd help me. Are you deserting me now?'

She flinched as if he'd struck her. 'If you go after Thiazzi, I'll have to. Someone has to warn the Open

Forest.' In her voice he heard an echo of Fin-Kedinn: the same flinty resolve to do what was right, no matter what the cost.

'Renn,' he said. 'I cannot turn around now. I need you to come with me. Do this for me.'

'Torak – I *can't!*'

He looked at her standing there with the black water swirling round her calves. 'Then that's how it is,' he said. Digging in his paddle, he started upriver.

TWENTY-SEVEN

Renn stood in the freezing shallows, staring blankly into the darkness.

She couldn't believe Torak was really gone. It was a mistake. It had to be. Any moment now and he'd reappear and say sorry. 'You're right. We've got to get back to the Open Forest.' He wouldn't just leave her.

But he had. She faced the long, dangerous journey without him.

And she was quite sure that he would never get near Thiazzi. How could he, when the Oak Mage held the Deep Forest in his fist? Thiazzi would kill him. She would never see Torak again.

A reed tapped her on the shoulder, and the willows murmured a warning. *Better get away from here, fast.*

Biting her lower lip hard, she squelched towards the

nearest dugout. She got behind it and pushed, but the heavy pine didn't budge. Slithering in the mud, she gave it another heave, and the boat jerked loose and splashed into the shallows.

Swiftly she tossed in quiver, bow and boots, and jumped in after them. But as she made the first stab with her paddle, the dugout tipped sharply, nearly throwing her out. She paddled frantically.

Shadowy hunters dragged her back to land.

'You helped the outcast get away,' said the Forest Horse Leader.

'Yes.'

'Where did he go?'

'B-back to the Open Forest.'

'You're in league with him.'

'He's my friend.'

'You're in league with him against the Deep Forest.'

'N-no.' Her teeth were chattering – the chill of the river was seeping into her marrow – but they wouldn't let her ashore. Scarred faces loomed over her, engulfing her in a stink of tallow, wet wovenbark and hate.

'You poisoned us with Magecraft,' said the Forest Horse Leader.

'No.'

'You put a sleeping-draught in our water.'

So she'd guessed rightly. But who had done it, and why?

'You put a spell on us!'

Renn hesitated. Taking credit for others' deeds had been her mother's skill. 'I warned you I was a Mage,' she said coldly. 'None of you was hurt. And none will be – if you take me to the Auroch Mage.'

The air crackled with fear and hatred. Renn prayed that their fear would prove the stronger.

'Why would we do that?' said the Forest Horse Leader.

'The Auroch Mage has the respect of all,' Renn said haughtily. 'I will speak only to him.'

'You're in no position to bargain,' hissed the Leader.

Renn thought fast. 'Is this how the Forest Horses respect the truce?' she said. 'By scorning the Auroch Mage? What do the Aurochs say about that?'

It was the turn of the Forest Horse Leader to hesitate.

The shelter of the Auroch Mage squatted like a toad in the lee of a fallen spruce.

The Aurochs had brought her here blindfold – by river, then overland – and she had no idea where she was, although she knew by the smell that she was close to the burnt lands.

'Our Mage is old and frail,' they'd warned her as they slipped off the blindfold, 'you mustn't tire him. And remember, you're only seeing him because he wishes it.' Then they'd vanished into the Forest, leaving her alone before the shelter.

She stood with her hands tied behind her back, in a tangle of deadnettle still damp with dew. Above her towered the tree's root disc, smelling of earth and rotting wood. It was pitted with the nests of bats and owls, and hung with auroch horns incised with spirals. From these and the encircling pines, slender ropes of red wovenbark trailed into the shelter's smoke-hole. Renn guessed they were spirit ladders, to help the Mage climb to the spirit world.

The shelter itself appeared oddly homely. A fragrant haze curled from the smoke-hole, and the wovenbark cloth across the doorway was decorated with a border of trotting aurochs.

'Come inside,' said a faint voice.

Awkwardly because of her bound hands, Renn got down on her knees, nosed aside the wovenbark, and shuffled in.

The fire was small, but welcoming. Above it, the red tails of the spirit ladders dangled through the smoke-hole, dancing in the heat. On the other side of the fire, Renn saw her bow and the stolen arrows lying beside a mound of leaves.

It shifted. 'I've sent my people away,' wheezed a voice as quiet as a summer breeze in a sapling. 'When two Mages meet, it's best if they're not overheard.'

Renn bowed respectfully. 'Mage.'

As her eyes adjusted to the gloom, she saw that the Mage was entirely covered in leaves. Layer on layer of fresh foliage – holly, birch, spruce, willow – feathered his robe in every shade of green. On his breast hung chunks of grass-coloured amber knotted on a nettlestem string. His hood was drawn low over his face – Renn couldn't see his eyes – but she felt his scrutiny.

'Why do you disturb my prayers?' he murmured, although without reproach.

Renn wondered how to begin. If the Auroch Mage was as fair as people said, and if he hadn't fallen wholly under Thiazzi's spell, she had a chance. If not . . .

'There's a Soul-Eater in the Deep Forest,' she blurted out.

'A *Soul-Eater*?'

'His name is Thiazzi. He set the Aurochs against the Forest Horses and now he's making them attack the Open

Forest.' She gulped. It was a huge relief to get it out.

The green robe rustled as the Mage reached for a stick and prodded the embers. Willow leaves at the hem curled in the heat, and Renn saw a beetle scramble for safety. 'This is grave news,' whispered the Mage. 'Who is this – *Thiazzi*?'

A small amber bead fell from a fold in his robe and rolled to the edge of the fire. Renn wondered if she ought to pick it up. 'He's the Oak Clan Mage,' she said. 'He killed the Forest Horse Mage. He took the place of their new Mage. The Mage you've been speaking to . . . he's not who you think.'

'No?' He sounded bemused. 'And – you've made all this out by yourself?'

'Yes,' Renn lied.

'Who are you?'

'I'm Renn. A Mage of the Raven Clan. I tried to warn the others, but they wouldn't listen.'

'And you came here to defeat the Soul-Eaters.'

'With your help, Mage.'

'Ah,' sighed the Mage, his chest gently heaving with each breath.

In the fire, the amber bead sizzled and flared. Renn caught a familiar tang. That's not amber, she thought. It's spruce-blood.

'To defeat the Soul-Eaters,' said the Mage, who seemed to be growing, filling the shelter. His chest heaved with laughter as he threw back his hood and shook out his russet mane. 'And how,' said Thiazzi, 'do you intend to do that?'

TWENTY-EIGHT

The Oak Mage was in no hurry to kill her.

Reaching into the sleeve of his robe, he brought out a handful of spruce-blood pellets and shook some into his mouth. Renn watched his yellow teeth grinding them to nothing. She saw a golden speck caught in the tangle of his beard. The truth settled upon her like snow. Thiazzi was the Auroch Mage *and* the Forest Horse Mage. He'd killed them both and taken their place, making use of the Forest Horse mask and the Auroch's solitary vigils. Soon one of them would disappear, and the other would rule alone.

Only Renn knew his secret. And he knew that she knew.

The yellow teeth went on grinding. The green eyes watched her lazily.

Kneeling before him with her hands tied behind her

back, she was utterly in his power. He spat a crumb at the fire and smiled to see her cringe. 'I suppose you're going to swear to me that you won't tell anyone.'

She tried not to tremble. 'No point,' she said.

His eyes gleamed. 'And no point pretending you're not terrified.'

She did not reply.

With awesome speed for so huge a man, he crossed to her side of the fire, engulfing her in rustling leaves and a stinging smell of spruce. His hand circled her throat: his three-fingered hand. Rough stumps searched her flesh till they found the vein. He grinned to feel her terror hammering under her skin. He could snap her neck like kindling. One twist, and it was the end.

Her thoughts darted like minnows. Say something. Anything. 'The – the fire-opal,' she gasped.

Out of the corner of her eye, she saw his free hand move to his chest. Had she imagined it, or did a shadow cross his face? But what could the Oak Mage possibly fear?

She took a leap in the dark. 'You haven't told her,' she said.

'Told who?' he replied a shade too quickly.

' – *Eostra*,' she whispered, and the name turned her voice as cold as the breath of a bone-mound. 'You haven't told her you've got it. But she knows. Oh, yes. The Eagle Owl Mage always knows. She's coming after you.'

His red tongue slid out and licked his lips. 'You can't possibly know that.'

'But I do. I have my mother's gift.'

'Your – mother?'

'Can't you see?' She met his gaze. 'The Viper Mage. I bear her marrow in my bones . . . I know what Eostra intends.'

'How could you know? You're not a Mage!'

'I know that the spirit walker has escaped,' she said, feeding on his unease. 'I know that your plans have gone awry. What's gone wrong? Who's turned against you?'

He threw her from him, and she hit her head on the doorpost. Dazed, she struggled upright. She heard him laugh.

'Yes,' he mused, 'maybe this way is better. Maybe live bait will be more effective than dead.'

From his sleeve he drew a jagged flint knife as long as Renn's forearm. She shrank from him, but he barely noticed. No time for pleasure now, he was intent on his work. Yanking a handful of spirit ladders through the smoke-hole, he severed them and used the rope to bind her ankles, then gagged her with bruising force.

He brought his face close to hers. 'You've got something to do before you die,' he breathed. 'You're going to give me the spirit walker.'

Wildly she shook her head.

'Oh yes. You're going to bring him to me at the sacred grove.'

After a brief, brutal search, he found her beaver-tooth knife and her grouse-bone whistle, cut the medicine pouch from her belt, and tossed all three on the fire. The last thing he did before casting his hood over his face was to take her bow in his hands and snap it in two.

TWENTY-NINE

Torak thought he saw Wolf on the bank, but when he called, he did not appear. Nor did the ravens. It was as if they knew what he'd done, and condemned him for it.

'But I didn't abandon her,' he said. '*She* left *me*.'

A gust of wind ruffled the river, and the alders stirred reproachfully. A gnarled oak scowled at him as he paddled by.

He could not believe that Renn had left him and gone back to the Open Forest. Surely she would change her mind and come after him? But when he listened for the sound of a dugout, all he heard was the gurgle of water and the sighs of slumbering trees.

She'll be all right, thought Torak. She can look after herself.

Oh, of course she can, Torak. Why would she need your help, hunted by hostile clans in the heart of the Deep Forest, with a Soul-Eater on the loose?

As dawn broke, he stopped for a rest and something to eat. Everything reminded him of Renn. The early morning sun trembled in a patch of wood strawberries. If she'd been with him, she would have dug up a couple of roots and chewed them to clean her teeth. As he groped in the shallows for reed stems and crunched them raw, he remembered a day last summer when she'd tried to feed one to Wolf, and it had turned into a game of tag. All three of them had ended up in the water, Torak and Renn helpless with laughter, while Wolf splashed about, worrying his prize and play-growling as if it were a lemming.

'*Enough!*' said Torak.

On the opposite bank, an otter raised her sleek head and stared at him, then went back to munching the trout in her forepaws.

Rek flew down, grabbed the otter's tail in her beak, and tugged. The outraged otter spun round, snarling at the intruder, and while her back was turned, Rip swooped and snatched the fish from her paws.

Both ravens alighted near Torak and demolished the fish. Sharing it, he noted, just as he and Renn shared everything. He struck the earth with his fist.

When nothing was left of the trout but bones, Rek flew onto Torak's shoulder and gently tugged his ear. Rip walked towards him and gazed at the medicine pouch at his belt: the swansfoot pouch which had been Renn's until she'd given it to him last spring.

'Not you too,' Torak told the ravens irritably.

Rip waggled his tail and stared at the pouch.

Without knowing why, Torak opened it and took out his

medicine horn. Both ravens tilted their heads, as if listening.

Moodily, Torak turned the horn in his fingers. It was carved with spiky marks which looked like spruce trees. Fin-Kedinn had once told Torak that this had been his mother's sign for the Forest, which was how he'd recognized the horn as hers. Now, Torak saw what he'd forgotten. Twisted round the tip of the horn was the strand of Renn's hair which he'd found in her sleeping-sack when he was outcast.

Slowly, he unwound it. Rip hopped onto his knee, took the hair in his beak, and ran it through his bill as delicately as if he were preening a feather.

Torak heaved a sigh. Renn had sent the ravens to help him last summer when he was soul-sick. And he'd abandoned her.

Just as he'd abandoned Bale.

The thought made him go cold. It was happening again. He'd quarrelled with Bale, and Bale had died. Now Renn . . .

His fist closed over the strand of hair. He would go back and find her. He would *make* her come with him. Vengeance must wait a little longer.

Jumping into the dugout, he turned it around and started downriver.

This time, the ravens flew with him.

Now Wolf was confused as well as worried. What was Tall Tailless doing?

Ever since the Bright Beast had eaten the Forest, Wolf had followed, and not understood. He'd prowled about the great Dens of the taillesses and watched them snarl at each other, then tear the strips of hide from their heads. Then they'd dragged in his pack-brother, and Wolf had been about to leap to his aid when Tall Tailless had snarled at *them*. That terrible, snarling blood-hunger . . . It was not-wolf. Wolf didn't understand it. It frightened him.

Then he'd followed Tall Tailless and the pack-sister to the Fast Wet, where *they* had snarled at each other, and then – *Tall Tailless had abandoned her.* A wolf does not abandon his pack-sister. Was Tall Tailless sick? Was his mind broken?

After that, Wolf had kept to the Dark as he'd followed his pack-brother up-Wet. Tall Tailless had called, but Wolf hadn't gone to him. Wolf *hated* hiding from his pack-brother, but he knew – with the certainty which came to him at times – that he could not go to him.

Although he didn't yet know why.

THIRTY

There must have been a storm in the Mountains, because the Blackwater bore Torak swiftly back to the Deep Forest camp.

Masking the dugout with leafy branches, he lay flat, trusting the reeds to conceal him. He was lucky. Everyone was hard at work, painting trees. He saw women, men and children laboriously smearing on earthblood.

What madness, he wondered, made them blindly follow orders? Couldn't they see that Thiazzi was stealing their freedom, like a fox raiding a carcass?

When the camp had drifted out of sight, he took up his paddle. The afternoon wore on. The west wind carried the stink of the wasteland. And still he found no sign of Renn.

As he rounded a bend, he saw that the north bank was muddied, as if by dugouts. The boats were gone, but something flashed on a willow branch. A lock of dark-red hair.

Landing the dugout, Torak made his way warily up the bank.

A swathe of men's tracks led into the Forest. Among them he found Renn's. She'd been re-captured. Why had they brought her here?

Forcing himself to concentrate, he worked out that the men had returned a short while later and paddled away. Had they taken Renn with them? He didn't think so.

Further in, he found another strand of her hair, tied to a twig. Then another. The tightness inside him unclenched a little. She must have been all right if she'd been able to do that. And she'd wanted him to follow.

Drawing his knife, he headed into the Forest.

Dusk was falling when he reached a small shelter in the lee of a fallen spruce. He saw slender scarlet ropes strung from trees, and auroch horns carved with sacred spirals. He guessed this was the prayer shelter of the Auroch Mage. But it had the peculiar stillness of an abandoned camp.

The doorway was barred by two crossed branches: one oak, one yew. Filled with misgiving, Torak stepped over them and went inside. The fire was dead white embers, crumbly as bones, but something lay across it. His belly turned over. It was the remains of Renn's bow.

In disbelief he took up the black, broken pieces of yew on which she had lavished so much care. He remembered a day last summer when he'd found her grinding hazelnuts to oil it. The sun had blazed in her red hair, and he'd wondered what would it feel like to wind it round his wrist. She'd turned and met his eyes, and his face had flamed. Wolf had nosed past him after the hazelnuts, and Renn had batted his muzzle away, 'No, Wolf, not for you!' But she'd soon relented and given him a handful.

Kneeling in the embers, Torak gripped the remains of the bow. He smelt ash, and the tang of spruce. By his knee, he saw a tiny amber pellet. He picked it up. Yes, spruce-blood. Beside it, a handprint. The hand of a large man. Missing two fingers.

Everything fell into place, and Torak spiralled down, down from a great height. Thiazzi was the Auroch Mage. Thiazzi was the Forest Horse Mage. They were one and the same.

And Thiazzi had Renn.

Lurching to his feet, Torak stumbled from the shelter. Moonlight washed the clearing in icy blue. He thought of Renn being forced to watch Thiazzi snap her bow in two. How the Soul-Eater must have enjoyed that. And he'd wanted Torak to know it. He'd left the bow as a sign, with his three-fingered handprint. *Thiazzi did this.*

It was Thiazzi, not Renn, who had left those strands of her hair on the trail: leading Torak here, making sure that he took the bait. And those crossed branches . . . Proclaiming where he'd taken her.

The sacred grove, where corpses dangled from the oak.

Torak staggered to a tree and retched.

This was his fault. In his hunger for vengeance, he had delivered Renn into the power of the Oak Mage.

Tall Tailless was only a pounce away, but Wolf couldn't go to him. Something was keeping them apart, like a great Fast Wet rushing between them.

Tall Tailless had been holding the pack-sister's Long

Claw-that-Flies in his forepaws, and now he put it carefully in the tree. Wolf sensed his fear, and underneath it, his terrible blood-urge.

It was the blood-urge which stopped Wolf going to him. *I have to kill the Bitten One*, Tall Tailless had once told Wolf. *Not because he is prey or in a fight over ranges, but because he killed the pale-pelted tailless.*

But *why*? This was not what a wolf does. This – this was not-wolf.

Worry clawed at Wolf's belly. He savaged a branch. He ran in circles.

Tall Tailless had heard him. He stooped and whined. *Come to me, pack-brother. I need you!*

Wolf whimpered. He backed away.

He remembered the time in the Great Cold when he'd found the white wolves, and had tried to tell their leader about Tall Tailless. *He has no tail*, Wolf had said, *and he walks on his hind legs, but he is . . .*

Then he is not-wolf, the lead wolf had sternly replied.

Wolf had known the leader was wrong, but he hadn't dared protest.

But now.

Tall Tailless rose on his hind legs and came towards Wolf, his face puzzled. *Why won't you come to me?*

His face . . .

From the beginning, Wolf had loved his pack-brother's flat, furless face; but as he stood in the Dark, staring up at it, he saw how different it was from that of a wolf. The eyes of Tall Tailless didn't throw back the light of the Bright White Eye, as the eyes of wolves do.

Not like a wolf.

It crashed upon Wolf with the force of a falling tree, the knowledge that had been stalking him for many Lights and Darks. Tall Tailless was not-wolf.

A pain such as Wolf had never known bit deep into his heart. Not even when he was a cub on the Mountain and missing Tall Tailless terribly, not even then had he felt such pain.

Tall Tailless was not-wolf.

Not wolf.

Tall Tailless was not wolf.

THIRTY-ONE

I thought you knew, said Torak in wolf talk.

Wolf backed away, his amber eyes clouded with misery.

Oh, Wolf. I thought you knew.

Whimpering, Wolf turned tail and fled.

Torak ran after him, crashing through the trees. It was hopeless. Lurching to a halt, he doubled up, gasping for breath. Around him, whitebeams unfurled their silver leaves to cup the light of the full moon. He howled. Wolf did not howl back. Torak's howl sank to a sob. Wolf was gone. Gone for ever?

The trees stirred in the wind, whispering, *Hurry, hurry*. Already, Thiazzi might have reached the sacred grove. He might have woken another fire and sunk a stake into its heart. He might be dragging Renn towards it . . .

Torak ran past the shelter, back to where he'd left the dugout. He jumped in and headed upstream, stabbing the river as if it were Thiazzi. He was in an endless tunnel of dark trees and hopeless thoughts. Because of him, Wolf was in misery. Because of him, Renn was in the power of the Oak Mage.

The Blackwater was implacable. His muscles burned. He deserved it.

Through the trees, he glimpsed the glow of the Deep Forest camp. But the river was barred. A wovenbark net stretched from bank to bank.

Jamming in his paddle, Torak drove the dugout back. When he was out of sight, he put in at a clump of alders and scrambled up the bank. He couldn't go any further by river, he'd have to go on foot. He'd never reach the sacred grove in time.

Suddenly, he froze. Through the soles of his boots, he caught a faint tremor in the earth.

He sank to his knees and placed both palms on the ground. Had he really felt it? Was it heading towards him?

Maybe, after all, there *was* a way.

Wolf felt the earth shudder beneath his paws, but still he loped. He smelt that he was heading towards the Bright Beast-bitten lands. He didn't care.

At last, thirst scratched his throat and he had to stop. He found a little Still Wet and snapped some up. Then he raised his muzzle and howled his misery to the Forest.

Tall Tailless was not wolf.

Tall Tailless was not Wolf's pack-brother.

Wolf no longer *had* a pack-brother.

Wolf was alone.

The shuddering beneath his pads grew stronger. Listlessly, Wolf recognized it as the pounding of many hooves.

To get out of the way, he trotted up a rise, from where he watched the horses gallop past. Their rich smell swirled about his nose, but he was too miserable to be tempted, or to wonder what was making them run.

When they'd gone, he slunk down to the little Still Wet again.

The earth around it had been chewed up by the horses' hooves, and it clung to his paws in cold, soggy lumps. He didn't care. He wondered if Tall Tailless would hear the horses in time to get out of the way. Tall Tailless who could hardly hear or smell at all, and who no longer had a pack-brother to warn him.

As Wolf stood with drooping tail at the edge of the Still Wet, he saw the wolf who lives in the Wet gazing up at him. This was a very odd wolf, who had no scent. That had frightened Wolf when he was a cub, but he'd soon learnt that the odd wolf meant no harm, and always drew back when he did.

Right now, the wolf in the Wet looked almost as miserable as Wolf felt. To cheer him up, Wolf gave a faint wag of his tail, and the wolf in the Wet wagged his tail, too.

Then a very strange thing happened. *Another* wolf appeared in the Wet, standing beside the first one.

Only this wolf was black.

THIRTY-TWO

Darkfur stood very still, waiting to see what Wolf would do.

Wolf, too, kept very still. His claws dug into the mud. His pelt tingled with excitement.

Darkfur twitched her tail.

Wolf lifted his muzzle and sniffed.

Slowly, Darkfur raised her foreleg and pawed his shoulder.

They touched noses.

Wolf seized her scruff in his jaws. She lashed her tail and whined, showing him her belly. He released her, and now they were rolling and tumbling in a muddy blur of fur and fangs. In and out of the Wet they chased each other, Wolf making fast little greeting snaps at her flanks, Darkfur whimpering with delight and snapping him back. She leapt high, her black pelt glittering with Wet, then twisted round and body-slammed him, and he chased her over the rise and down again, snuffing her fierce, strong scent, the most beautiful scent he'd ever smelt.

Now she was pawing some leaves off the Wet and they were snapping it up, then slumping together for a rest. Panting, she told him how she'd missed him, so she'd left the pack to find him. After many Lights and Darks and much sniffing and listening, she'd howled for him and thought he'd howled back, but then the Bright Beast had eaten all the scents.

Wolf shut his eyes and heard the soft wind ruffling her fur. He felt surprised and happy and sad.

Darkfur was clever, and quick to sense what he was feeling. *Why are you sad?* she asked. *Where is the one who has no tail?*

Wolf jumped up and shook himself. *He is not wolf. He is not my pack-brother.*

Darkfur twitched one ear in puzzlement. *But we played together. He was your pack-brother. This can't be.*

Wolf trotted back and forth. He found an interesting stick and dropped it before her as a present.

Darkfur ignored it. She rose and nose-nudged his shoulder. *Do you remember when the cubs tried to eat his overpelt and you stopped them? And I gave him a fish-head?*

The pain was so bad that Wolf whined. Of course he remembered that shining day when he and Tall Tailless had been part of the Mountain pack; when they had swum together and been happy.

Darkfur rubbed her rump against his shoulder and nuzzled his scruff. *I've been chasing horses. There's a juicy little foal. I nearly caught it but its mother kicked. Let's hunt!*

Wolf turned his muzzle into the wind, and the horse

192

scent flowed over his nose. The herd must have halted as soon as Darkfur stopped chasing. It wasn't far off.

Darkfur bounded into the trees, wagging her tail. *Come!* Then she was loping after the horses, a sleek black wolf flying through the nettles.

Hunger woke up in Wolf's belly. He forgot his pain and raced after her.

Torak felt the tremor of hooves through the earth. The horses were heading his way. Something must have panicked them, maybe a lynx or a bear. Good, he thought. The faster the better.

Now he could hear them. As they came closer, he caught huffing and blowing and the breaking of branches. He moved off the trail, flattening himself against a beech tree.

Moments later, the lead mare burst into view. Her head was up, her tail flying. She sped past and the herd raced after her, a glossy black river of straining necks and powerful haunches.

As soon as they'd passed, Torak gave a piercing whinny.

He heard the slap of horseflesh on horseflesh as they skittered into one another; then an answering whinny.

Torak stepped onto the trail and waited.

Bracken stirred. He heard a snort. A stamp. A sleek black head pushed through.

The lead mare halted twenty paces away from him. Her flanks were heaving, her nostrils flared.

He nickered to reassure her.

She tossed her head.

In a low, gentle tone, he began to talk. 'You've smelt me

before, remember? I helped a foal back to the herd. You know I mean no harm.'

Her ears swivelled to catch his voice, but her head stayed nervously high, and she swung her hindquarters round towards him. *Stay back. I kick!*

Slowly he walked towards her, talking, not taking his gaze from her, but not alarming her with a direct stare.

Steam rose from her flanks. Her great dark eyes were wide, but no longer rimmed with white. For an instant, Torak met her gaze, and a current of knowledge flowed between them. His souls had hidden in her marrow. He had known what it was to be horse. And she knew that he knew.

'I know,' he said, moving nearer. 'I know.'

She side-stepped and swished her tail. No man had ever got this close.

He felt the heat from her flanks. He bent and sniffed her nostrils, as he'd seen horses do in greeting, and she let him, her grassy breath warming his face. Placing his hand lightly on her shoulder, he pinched his thumb and fingers together and scratched the sweaty pelt, mimicking the nibble-greetings of a horse.

A shiver rippled from her withers to her tail, and she gave a snorty blow of pleasure.

'I'm your friend,' he told her. 'You know that, don't you?'

Still finger-nibbling, he worked his way up her neck, and she turned her head and gently nipped his shoulder, returning the greeting.

His hand moved down to her withers, and he grasped a handful of mane.

Then he did what no-one in all the clans had ever done before.

He vaulted onto her back.

THIRTY-THREE

The mare gave an outraged squeal and did her best to buck Torak off. He clung to her mane and hooked his legs in front of her belly.

She reared – maybe *that* would rid her of this infuriating burden – but he flung himself forwards and gripped with his thighs.

She launched into a gallop, nearly wrenching his arms from their sockets. He slithered about on her broad, slippery back, just managing to stay on.

She made for a low-hanging branch. He ducked. Twigs scraped his back. He stayed low in case she tried that again.

They crashed through thickets, and the herd – panicked by her panic – crashed after them. Between the trees, Torak glimpsed the river. The mare was heading upstream towards the valley where she felt safe.

Her hide was rough against his cheek, and as he smelt her horsey sweat and heard her breath sawing in her chest, he felt a pang of guilt. She was his friend and he'd frightened her. Too bad. Nothing mattered except saving Renn.

Without warning, the mare's forequarters rose, her withers smashing into his cheekbone, and for a moment they were flying over a fallen tree. Then the mare thudded to earth, bashing his cheek again.

Seeing spots, he scrambled upright as they sped into the glare of firelight, into the heart of the Deep Forest camp. Trampling pails and cooking-skins, they galloped between the scarlet trees, while around them people scattered, snatching up children and gaping at Torak.

Over his shoulder he shouted, 'Your Mage is a Soul-Eater in disguise! Come to the sacred grove and see for yourselves!' Then the camp was behind them and they were racing uphill towards the ridge.

Only then did Torak realize that no-one had shot at him. No arrows, no poisoned darts. They dared not risk harming the sacred herd. His medicine pouch banged against his thigh, and without knowing why, he thanked his mother's spirit for keeping him safe.

Another fallen tree rushed towards him, and he threw himself against the mare's neck just before she jumped. Mud splattered his face as she landed in a bog, sinking up to her hocks. She struggled to free herself, and he leaned forwards to help her. Her hindquarters gave a tremendous heave and they were out, flushing grouse from the rushes in a gobbling flurry.

The moon was sinking, the shadows leaching from the Forest as they hurtled towards the Windriver. Torak saw that they were further east than the trail he'd taken before; this way was steeper, more overgrown. The wily mare knew a shortcut to her valley.

Branches tore at his hair, blackthorn blossom flew like snow. Suddenly, the mare jolted to a trot, then halted altogether, throwing down her head and nearly pitching him over her withers. Behind her, the herd ran into each other, shook themselves, and began to graze.

'No!' panted Torak, flapping his legs and punching her neck. 'Don't stop, we're not there yet!' It was useless. The mare scarcely felt it. When he went on punching, she stamped and lashed her tail, catching him stingingly on the cheek. She was on her own ground now, and not to be intimidated.

Or not by Torak.

A familiar cark! overhead, and Rip and Rek swooped, their talons almost grazing the mare's rump, before flicking skywards.

Startled, she jerked up her head, and behind her the herd snorted in alarm.

Again the ravens swooped. The mare side-stepped, showing the whites of her eyes. But it wasn't only the ravens, Torak realized. She'd caught a scent she feared.

Once again, she broke into a canter. Once again, they crashed through the willows. The mare was tiring and so was Torak. His limbs ached, and he rode in a blur of black branches and raven wings.

The Windriver vanished underground, and willows gave way to spruce. In the east, Torak saw a red sliver of dawn, livid as a wound.

The mare's hoofbeats sounded loud as they entered the holly trees, and Torak felt the power of Thiazzi swirling around him. The mare didn't like the hollies. But whatever had spooked her still drove her on.

She smelt the fire before he did. Then Torak saw it: black smoke piercing the bloody sky. Dread became a stone in his belly. Was he too late?

He put his hand to the pouch at his belt and felt the medicine horn. He had no breath left to pray out loud, but in his head he prayed to his mother to save Renn. He prayed to the World Spirit. He called upon Wolf.

As Wolf and Darkfur loped after the horses, Wolf sensed that their hunt was changing its purpose, although he didn't know what it was.

He slowed to a trot, and Darkfur slowed with him. He pricked his ears. On the wind he caught a faint, high keening: higher than the highest wolf whine or the sharpest bat-squeak.

Darkfur heard it too, but she didn't recognize it. Wolf did. It was the yowl of the deer bone which Tall Tailless carried at his flank. The deer bone which used to be silent, but had now begun to sing.

With it, Wolf caught another sound, but this was one that Darkfur couldn't hear, as it was inside Wolf's head. It was Tall Tailless howling for him; just as Wolf had howled for Tall Tailless in his head long ago, in that terrible time when the bad taillesses had trapped him in the stone Den. *Pack-brother! Come to me! The pack-sister is in danger!*

A cold nose nudged Wolf's flank. Darkfur was puzzled. *Why do you slow?*

Wolf didn't know what to do. *He is not wolf*, he told her.

Darkfur's gaze turned stern. *You were pack-brothers. A wolf does not abandon his pack-brother.*

Wolf stood miserably on the trail, listening to the howling in his head, while the Great Bright Eye peered above the Mountains, and the scent of the Bright Beast-that-Bites-Hot flew towards him on the wind.

THIRTY-FOUR

The stink of burnt meat sickened Renn.

'Next time it's you,' Thiazzi had told her. She hadn't made a sound, but he'd laughed just the same.

After the nightmare journey in the dugout, he had slung her over his shoulder and strode off through the Forest. She'd swung like a sack, her face banging into his back at every stride.

She'd known at once when they'd reached the sacred grove, because the trees felt intensely aware. They'd watched, but they hadn't helped. To them she was as insignificant as dust.

The Soul-Eater had carried her through a wall of thorns and past the embers of a great round fire. He'd climbed a pine trunk notched with footholds which stood propped against an enormous tree. Renn had seen peeling bark and caught the scent of yew. She'd tried not to think of her bow. Then Thiazzi was thrusting aside branches and throwing her down, and she was falling into the Great Yew's cavernous heart.

Her wrists and ankles throbbed and her shoulders ached from being pinioned for so long. Her mouth hurt from the gag, but she couldn't chew it because Thiazzi had tied it so tight. Worst of all, she'd landed with her left leg twisted under her, and whenever she moved, pain shot through her knee.

All through the endless night she'd huddled in the dark, listening to her panicky breath. To keep up her courage, she'd told herself that somewhere above, the full moon was shining. Then it had occurred to her that soon its strength would wane, when the sky bear caught it and began to feed.

For the first time in her life, she had nothing to wish for. She couldn't wish for Torak to come, because Thiazzi would kill him. But if he didn't come, Thiazzi would kill her.

Around her rose the gaunt flanks of the Great Yew: fissured, flaking, fiercely alive. She shifted to ease her cramped limbs, crunching owl pellets and bones beneath her, some large, some brittle and delicate as frost. She thought, I'm lying on the remains of thousands of winters.

Far above, unreachably far, a patch of sky slowly bled from grey to red, and a last star glimmered. She craned to see it, and by her knee, a spider scuttled for safety. She wished it would come back. She didn't want to be alone.

She ached for her bow. For so many summers it had been part of her, a silent friend who'd never let her down. In her head, she heard again that terrible snap.

Now she had nothing. No knife, no axe, no medicine

201

horn. No whistle for calling Wolf, no means of summoning Rip and Rek. She was going to die here, alone. Unavenged.

She slumped against the yew, and something dug into her forearm. It was her wrist-guard. At least, she thought, I still have that.

It was polished greenstone, very smooth and beautiful. Fin-Kedinn had made it for her when he'd taught her to shoot. The thought of him was a blaze of light in the darkness. She would *not* die unavenged. Fin-Kedinn would find out, and then Thiazzi had better beware. When the Raven Leader was angry, it was worse than any Soul-Eater. Renn pictured the lines of her uncle's face hardening to carved sandstone; his vivid, blue, freezing stare. She sat straighter.

Fin-Kedinn said that a hunter's most precious possession was not his strike-fire or his weapons, it was the knowledge he carried in his head.

Think, Renn told herself. Think.

The smell of smoke made her head throb. It was hard to order her thoughts.

The smoke.

It wasn't coming from above; that patch of sky was clear. But it had to be coming from somewhere.

After a painful circuit of the yew, she found several cracks: none wider than a finger, but at least she might be able to see what was going on.

This small victory of reason over dread made her feel a little better. Rising awkwardly to her feet and trying to favour her good leg, she hopped to the largest crack and peered through.

She saw the fire with its terrible offering. Behind it, very close, the trunk of an enormous oak. Bark faces leered at her, but the branches were blighted and barren.

Renn's heart jerked. Against the oak stood the pine-trunk ladder. Thiazzi hadn't left it against the yew, as she'd thought. So even if, by some amazing feat, she managed to free her hands and ankles and climb to that patch of sky, she would probably break her neck trying to get down.

And even if she didn't . . . Beyond the oak was the wall of thorns: juniper boughs piled chest-high, encircling the fire and the sacred trees. Thiazzi had closed the ring when he'd carried her in. If anyone came, they wouldn't be able to reach her; and she wouldn't be able to get out.

As she peered through the crack, a shadow cut across it. She recoiled and fell, jolting her knee and squealing in pain.

Thiazzi laughed. 'Not long now.'

Grimly, she struggled back to the crack.

The Oak Mage crossed in and out of sight as he circled the fire. He still wore his mantle of leaves, but his hood was thrown back to let his long hair flow free, and on his chest he wore his clan-creature wreath of acorns and mistletoe. The berries were the misty white of blinded eyes. Nestled among them, Renn saw a small black pouch.

The fire-opal.

She knew that Thiazzi felt her scrutiny and relished it, but she couldn't tear herself away. She watched him feed more branches to the fire. She stared at the charred meat dangling from the stake.

She forced her gaze upwards. The star had been snuffed out. *No help for you here*, taunted the empty sky.

Her mind scuttled like a spider. Where were Rip and Rek? And Wolf? And Torak?

No. *Don't* pray for him to come, that's what Thiazzi

wants. You're the bait. If he comes, you'll have to watch him die.

And Thiazzi would win, she had no doubt of that. He was the strongest man in the Forest, and he had a Mage's cunning.

The throbbing in her head was worse. With a jolt, she realized that she could no longer see her boots. Smoke was seeping through the cracks, pooling about her ankles.

Her eyes began to smart. She tried to cough, but only managed a muffled splutter through the gag.

'Not long now,' repeated Thiazzi.

Again she peered through the crack. The Oak Mage stood with legs braced, tossing a rawhide whip from palm to palm. His harsh features were taut with anticipation. What had he heard that she had not?

The noise in her head grew louder.

It wasn't in her head, it was outside, beyond the ring of thorns.

It was the pounding of horses' hooves.

THIRTY-FIVE

Nearer came the thundering hooves, and Renn pressed her face against the crack, straining to see.

A shadow at the corner of her eye, then a black horse was soaring over the thorns, with Torak – yes, *Torak* – on its back. In one hand he grasped the horse's mane, in the other his blue slate knife. His dark hair flew, and his face was stern and intent on Thiazzi.

The mare's hooves struck the ground, raising spurts of ash, but Torak clung on, his eyes never leaving the Oak Mage – who stood silent, tapping his whip against his thigh.

The mare snorted and tossed her head. Torak jumped from her back, staggered, but stood firm. The mare flicked up her tail and leapt the thorns again, and her hoofbeats faded to nothing.

Renn heard the crackle of the fire and the settling of ash. She ground her cheek against unyielding wood. *No, Torak, he'll kill you!* she wanted to scream.

With unhurried ease, Thiazzi cast off his mantle. Beneath it he wore the hides of many hunters – fox, lynx, wolverine, bear – and their strength was his strength, and from his belt hung his massive knife, its edge stained dull red from many kills. He was invincible: no longer a creature of leaves and bark, no longer *of* the Forest, but its ruler.

Torak stood glaring at him. 'Where is she?' he shouted.

'Where is she?' panted Torak. He was exhausted. His legs were trembling. It was a struggle to stay on his feet.

The Oak Mage faced him through the smoke: huge, silent, in control. Torak could see no sign of Renn. Only the pine-trunk ladder against the blighted oak, and the horror on the stake.

'This is what you wanted, isn't it?' he demanded. 'You wanted me. Well, here I am! Let her go!'

'And what do *you* want, Spirit Walker?' said Thiazzi. 'Revenge for your dead kinsman? Well, here *I* am. You have only to come and take it, and your oath will be fulfilled.' Baring his yellow teeth, he spread his arms, displaying the awesome might of his shoulders and chest.

Torak hesitated.

'If you so much as scratch my hand, Spirit Walker, the Raven girl dies. But if you give yourself into my power, she goes free.'

The fire hissed. The holly trees, the Great Oak and the Great Yew, all waited to see what Torak would do.

Without taking his gaze from Thiazzi, he unslung his quiver and bow, drew back his arm, and flung them over the thorns. His axe went next. Last of all, he hefted the blue slate knife which had been his father's, and threw it after them.

Weaponless, he faced the Soul-Eater through the shimmering heat. 'I renounce my vengeance,' he said. 'I break my oath. Take me. Let her live.'

THIRTY-SIX

'Let her live,' repeated Torak, but his voice had sunk to a pleading whisper. Dread seized him. Maybe Renn was already dead.

Thiazzi saw it in his face, and his lip curled. 'It's all for nothing, Oathbreaker. You'll never see your girl again.'

For an instant, Torak despaired.

Then, small and bright, he remembered Renn standing in the mouth of the cave, shooting her last arrows at the demon bear. She had known that she couldn't win, but she'd gone on fighting.

He lifted his head. 'I don't believe you.'

The Soul-Eater's whip crackled out, loosing a shower of sparks from the fire. 'It's over, Spirit Walker. Against me you have no power.'

'I'm not dead yet,' said Torak.

Thiazzi drew his knife and moved towards him.

Torak circled to escape.

The Oak Mage laughed. 'I'm going to rip out your spine. I'm going to grind your skull beneath my heel till your eyeballs burst. No more Spirit Walker buzzing round me like a gnat round a bison. I am the Oak Mage! *I* rule the Forest!' Foam flew from his lips. His voice echoed from the rocks.

Somewhere, a wolf howled. Two short howls. *Where — are you?*

Torak howled back. *I'm here! Where is the pack-sister?*

But Wolf didn't know.

Snarling, Thiazzi shook his three-fingered fist. 'Your wolf got a chunk of me once, but not this time!' Sheathing his knife, he snatched a brand from the fire and swept it round the ring of thorns. The juniper caught with a *wssh* — and became a wall of flame. Thiazzi was exultant. 'Even the fire does my will!'

Beyond the blazing wall, Torak heard a rattle of pebbles, then furious snarls and a yelp which ended in a whine. The flames were too high. He barked a warning. *Stay back! You can't help me!*

He put his hand to his medicine pouch — the swansfoot pouch which Renn had given him. 'Renn!' he shouted. 'Renn, where *are* you?'

Torak was shouting her name, but Renn only managed a squeal which ended in a cough. The Great Yew was full of smoke. If she didn't do something soon, it would become her death tree.

And yet — she couldn't tear herself from the crack. She felt that by watching, she was keeping Torak alive; if she looked away, Thiazzi would kill him.

Stupid, stupid! she told herself. But still she watched as Torak circled the fire and Thiazzi came after him: slowly, cracking his whip, playing with his prey as a lynx plays with a lemming. Torak was exhausted. His hair was stringy with sweat and he kept stumbling. He wasn't going to last much longer.

With a huge effort of will, Renn tore her gaze away. Shuffling backwards, her boots scuffed leafmould and bones, useless, crumbling bones. She fell, landing on her hands, hurting her palms. It was hopeless.

Warmth trickled between her fingers. She twisted round, but couldn't get far enough to see.

She'd cut her hand on a bone or a root. If she could find it again . . .

The smoke was too thick. She couldn't breathe, couldn't see. She groped behind her. Where *was* it?

There. A thin, jagged edge. Surely not flint? Whatever it was, it seemed to be wedged immovably in the yew.

Shuffling closer, she began sawing at the bindings round her wrists.

Sounds from outside were muffled and remote. Was that a wolf's yelp? A raven's caw? Through her rasping breath, she caught Thiazzi's mocking tones, but nothing from Torak.

She went on sawing at the rope.

The ravens wheeled and cawed, and for a moment Thiazzi glanced up. Torak seized his chance, grabbed a branch from the fire, and lashed out.

The Oak Mage dodged it easily, and Torak saw that his branch wasn't burning, it was a lifeless grey stump.

'You can't use fire against me,' sneered Thiazzi. 'I am Master of Forest *and* fire!'

As if in answer, a gust of wind stirred the trees, blinding Torak with smoke.

Again Rip swooped. Thiazzi's whip caught his wing, and though Rip soared to safety, a black feather drifted onto the embers.

The smoke made Torak cough. When he stopped, the coughing went on.

Thiazzi saw him falter, and his eyes glittered with malice. 'The fire can't hurt *me*, but it'll only take smoke to kill your girl.'

Wildly, Torak cast about him. Where was the coughing coming from? But the wind was gusting more strongly, he couldn't tell.

Thiazzi darted a glance at the Great Oak.

Of course. The ladder. The oak must be hollow. *Renn was inside the oak.*

Edging round the fire, Torak moved closer – and raced for the ladder.

To his surprise, the Oak Mage simply watched. When Torak was halfway up, he called out. 'Not as clever as you think you are, Spirit Walker. Now I've got you like a squirrel up a tree, while she chokes to death.'

Torak gripped the ladder. Thiazzi had tricked him. The coughing wasn't louder, it was fainter. It wasn't coming from the oak, but from the yew.

Shakily, he wiped the sweat from his face. 'Don't wait too long,' he panted with a desperate show of defiance. 'The clans are on their way . . . And you don't have your mask. They'll see you for what you really are.'

'Then I'll make it quick,' said Thiazzi. Striding to the foot of the ladder, he started to climb.

THIRTY-SEVEN

The wrist-bindings snapped. Renn yanked the gag over her chin, swallowed a chestful of smoke, and coughed till she retched. Frantically, she sawed at the bindings round her ankles, then struggled to her feet and hopped to the crack.

She couldn't see for smoke, couldn't hear Wolf or the ravens – or Torak. Don't think about it. Get out, get out.

Groping through the haze, she sought for footholds, handholds, anything to help her climb. Her fingers found something jutting above her head. It felt like a peg. It couldn't be. It was. She swung herself up, her good foot scrabbling for a hold. She found a dent barely deep enough for her toes. Her free hand clawed wood. *Another* peg. Someone had hammered them in, someone taller than her, she had to stretch to reach; and the yew seemed to be helping, leading her from peg to peg. Or maybe it just wanted her gone.

The top was the hardest, as the pegs ran out and the edge was rotten. Grabbing a branch, she hauled herself over and hung half in, half out. She'd scraped her fingers raw, and a broken branch was digging into her belly, but she was clear of the smoke, gulping the cool green breath of the Forest.

She was dizzyingly high up. No boughs below, and too far to jump. Trying not to jar her knee, she thrust aside branches. They sprang back in her face as if to say, *We helped you once, don't push your luck.* Then she saw Torak.

He was almost level with her, having cleared the top of the ladder and climbed onto one of the oak's outstretched arms. He didn't see her, he was straining to push the ladder away, while Thiazzi, still on it, held firm to both ladder and tree.

It was a battle Torak couldn't win. Renn watched helplessly as Thiazzi pulled himself onto a branch and reached round the bole of the tree. Torak dodged – and caught sight of Renn. His mouth shaped her name as he took in her predicament: trapped, no way to get down. Thiazzi darted round the other side to grab him. Torak dodged, seized the ladder, and heaved. Renn saw the pine trunk tilt towards her and crash into the yew, striking it halfway up the trunk. Torak had given her a way down.

It nearly cost him his life. As he reached for the next branch, Thiazzi lunged. Torak swung himself out of the way an instant too late, and Thiazzi's blade caught his thigh. Snarling in pain, he stamped on Thiazzi's wrist and sent the knife flying.

An empty victory. Renn could see that he didn't have a chance. The Soul-Eater didn't need weapons, he would climb after Torak till he reached the uppermost branch, and then . . .

She tore her gaze away. She couldn't help him from here, she had to get down.

The pine-trunk ladder was too far below, she'd have to jump onto it. Twisting round, she lowered herself over the edge till she was hanging by her hands, and let go. The pine shuddered as she struck it with her good foot, but it held. She didn't bother with the notches, she simply slid, scraping her hands and landing in a blaze of agony on her injured knee. When she looked, Torak was gone.

No – there he was, clinging to the oak's tapering bole. The Soul-Eater was gaining on him. Renn saw Thiazzi stretch to grab Torak's leg. He missed by a finger. Torak was nearly at the crown, where the tree branched for the last time. Renn saw him dark against the stormy sky, turning his head, wondering what to do. She pictured the Oak Mage seizing him by the ankle, hurling him screaming to his death.

Setting her teeth, she crawled towards the fire, dragging her bad leg. She grabbed a pine knot full of tree-blood, fiercely ablaze. She crawled towards the oak.

'Torak!' Her voice came out as a reedy gasp. *'Torak!'* she yelled. *'Catch!'*

His head whipped round.

Kneeling on her good leg, Renn drew back her arm to take aim. This had to be the finest throw of her life.

The burning brand spun through the air in a flurry of sparks – and Torak caught it.

Hanging on with his free hand, he lashed out at Thiazzi.

The Soul-Eater dodged behind the bole of the oak – reached round – and would have grabbed Torak's foot if his clan-creature wreath hadn't snagged on a branch, jerking him back. He tore it off, raining acorns and mistletoe, but clutching the fire-opal pouch to his breast.

That gave Torak a moment to scramble higher. He reached the crown and edged onto the sturdiest branch. It sagged beneath him. He made a swipe with the brand. The Oak Mage struck it a blow with his fist that nearly broke Torak's wrist and sent the brand flying. Time stopped as Torak watched his last chance spin in a trail of sparks and thud to earth.

Thiazzi was exultant. *'I am the Master!'* he roared.

But as he bellowed his triumph, the breath of the Forest blew a spark into the tangle of his hair. Torak saw it catch. The Oak Mage did not.

Desperately, Torak tried to distract him. 'You'll never be Master,' he taunted. 'Even if you kill me, you'll never get what you want!'

'And what's that?' sneered the Oak Mage, climbing closer.

'What you killed my kinsman for: the fire-opal.'

'But I have it!' Gloating, he brandished the pouch.

A bolt of black feathers shot from the sky and Rek made a grab for it, but Thiazzi brushed her aside with a sweep of his arm.

The laughter froze on his lips as a shadow slid over him. The eagle owl scythed the air with silent wings, swung her talons forwards, and ripped the pouch from his hand. Howling in fury, he reached for her, but she was gone, winging her way towards the High Mountains.

Now Thiazzi's howl became a scream, for the fire had taken hold, and it was hungry. Clawing at his mane, his beard, his clothes, he faltered – lost his balance – and fell.

High in the oak, Torak saw the Soul-Eater lying lifeless on the roots. He saw a throng of Deep Forest hunters emerge from the hollies, break through the ring of thorns, and surround the corpse. Then the clouds burst and the rain lashed down, quenching the flames and sending up plumes of bitter smoke; and the Forest gave a vast, shuddering sigh, having purged itself of the evil which had threatened its green heart.

Rain streamed down Torak's face as he climbed to safety, but he scarcely noticed. He was shaking with fatigue, yet strangely numb. He couldn't even feel the wound in his thigh.

Jumping to earth, he staggered to Renn, who was slumped by the ruins of the fire. Kneeling beside her, he gripped her shoulders. 'Are you hurt? Did he hurt you?'

She shook her head, but she was white as bone, and her eyes were shadowed with a darkness Thiazzi had created. She opened her mouth to say something; then her face worked and she twisted away from him. The nape of her neck was smooth and defenceless. He put his arms around her and pulled her close.

As they clung together, the medicine horn at his hip began to hum. Raising his head, he saw Wolf standing between the Great Yew and the Great Oak, his eyes glowing with the amber light of the guide. *Watch*, he told Torak. *It comes . . .*

From nowhere, a fierce wind swept through the sacred grove, whipping branches but making no sound. The sun rent the clouds, the great trees blazed so green that it hurt to look, but Torak could not avert his eyes. The humming of the horn was deep inside him, thrilling through his bones. The world splintered and fell away. He couldn't hear the sizzle of embers or the hiss of rain. He couldn't smell the smoke, or feel Renn in his arms.

In the drifting haze between the oak and the yew stood a tall man. His face was dark against the dazzling sky, and his long hair floated in the voiceless wind. From his head rose the antlers of a stag.

With a cry, Torak covered his eyes with his hand.

When he dared look again, the vision was gone, and there was Wolf, his pack-brother, wagging his tail and bounding towards him through the rain.

THIRTY-EIGHT

When Torak woke up, he didn't know where he was.

He lay beneath a mantle of warm hare fur. Green sunlight shone through a spruce-bough roof. He smelt woodsmoke, and heard the sounds of a camp: the crackle of a fire, the little grinding crunches of someone sharpening a knife.

Then it started coming back. Kneeling with Renn in the sacred grove. The Deep Forest clans crowding round; someone pressing his knife into his hands. The journey to camp, on foot and in a dugout. A woman sewing up the wound in his thigh, another poulticing Renn's knee. A honeyed drink which made him drowsy, then – nothing.

Shutting his eyes, he curled into a ball. There was a faint ache in his chest, as if something were trying to get out, and he had a gnawing feeling of apprehension. Thiazzi was dead; but Eostra had the fire-opal. And he and Renn were at the mercy of the Deep Forest clans.

When he emerged from the shelter, he found a throng of people waiting. They bowed low. He did not bow back. Two days before, they'd been baying for his blood.

To his surprise, he spotted Durrain and the Red Deer among them, with a few Willow and Boar Clan, but no Ravens. Where was Renn? He was about to ask when the Forest Horse Leader made an even deeper bow, and bade him come to the scarlet tree and wait.

Wait for what? he wondered. Around him the Deep Forest clans stared in unnerving silence.

It was a huge relief to see Renn hobbling towards him on crutches. 'Do you know,' she said in an undertone, 'you've slept a whole day and a night? I had to prod you to make sure you were still alive.' Her voice was brisk, but he saw that something was wrong, although she wasn't yet ready to tell him.

'Everyone keeps bowing,' he said under his breath.

'Nothing you can do about that,' she replied. 'You rode the sacred mare and fought the Soul-Eater. *And* the Great Oak is coming into leaf. They're saying you made it happen.'

He didn't want to talk of that, so he asked about her knee, and she shrugged and said it could be worse. He asked why Durrain was here, and Renn told him that the Deep Forest clans had rejected the Way as fiercely as they'd adopted it, and that they no longer scorned the Red Deer, who'd never followed it at all. 'And the Aurochs are so ashamed of having been tricked by a Soul-Eater that they mean to punish themselves with lots more scars. And nobody's going to attack the Open Forest.'

'Is that why the Boars and Willows are here, too?'

Her shoulders rose, and she stabbed the earth with her crutch. 'Fin-Kedinn sent them,' she said in a taut voice. 'He had a struggle preventing Gaup and his clan from attacking, but in the end he persuaded them to send only their Leader: to talk, not fight. The Willows and Boars came with them for support.'

'And Fin-Kedinn?' Torak said quickly.

She chewed her lip. 'Fever. He was too ill to come. That was a few days ago. No-one's heard anything since.'

There was nothing he could say to make that better, but he was about to try when the crowd parted and two Auroch hunters approached, dragging the ash-haired woman between them.

They released her and she stood swaying, peering at Torak with lashless eyes.

The Forest Horse Leader forced her to her knees at the point of her spear, and addressed the throng. 'Here is the sinner we caught near our camp!' she cried. 'She confessed. She was the one who released the great fire.' She bowed to Torak, her horsetail sweeping the ground. 'It's for you to decide punishment.'

'Me?' said Torak. 'But – if anyone, it should be Durrain.' He glanced at the Red Deer Mage, but she remained inscrutable.

'Durrain says you must do it,' said the Leader. 'All the clans agree. You saved the Forest. Decide the sinner's fate.'

Torak regarded the prisoner, who was watching him intently. This woman had tried to burn him alive. And yet he felt only pity. 'The Master is dead,' he told her. 'You do know that, don't you?'

'How I envy him,' she said with weary longing. 'He knew the fire at last.' Suddenly, she smiled at Torak, baring her broken teeth. 'But you – you are blessed! The fire let you live! I will submit to your judgement.'

Beside him, Renn stirred. 'It was you,' she said to the woman. 'You put the sleeping-potion in their water.'

The woman twisted her dry red hands. 'The fire let him live! They had no right to kill him.'

Angry murmurs from the crowd, and the Forest Horse Leader shook her spear. 'Speak the word,' she told Torak, 'and she dies.'

Torak looked from the vengeful green face to the ash-haired woman. 'Leave her alone,' he said.

There was a storm of protest.

'But she drugged us!' cried the Forest Horse Leader. 'She released the great fire! She *must* be punished!'

Torak turned on her. 'Are you wiser than the Forest?'

'Of course not! But –'

'Then this is how it will be! The Red Deer will keep watch on her always, and she will swear never to release the fire again.' He met the Leader's gaze and held it, and at last she lowered her spear. 'It shall be as you say,' she muttered.

'Ah,' breathed the crowd.

Durrain stood motionless, observing Torak.

Suddenly he wanted to be rid of them all, these wild-eyed people with their caked heads and scarlet trees.

As he pushed through the crowd, Renn hobbled after him. 'Torak, wait!'

He turned.

'You did the right thing,' she said.

'They don't know that,' he said in disgust. 'They'll let her live because I told them to. Not because it's right.'

'That won't matter to her.'

'Well it matters to me.'

He left her and headed out of camp. He didn't care

where he went, just as long as it was away from the Deep Forest clans.

He hadn't gone far before the wound in his thigh began to hurt, so he flung himself down on the riverbank and watched the Blackwater glide by. The ache in his chest was worse, and he wanted Wolf, but Wolf didn't come, and he didn't have the heart to howl.

He sensed someone behind him, and turned to see Durrain. 'Go away,' he growled.

She came closer and sat down.

He tore off a dock leaf and started shredding it along the veins.

'Your decision was wise,' she said. 'We will watch her well.' She paused. 'We didn't know how far her wits had wandered. We were wrong to give her so much freedom. We – made a mistake.'

Torak wished Renn could have heard that.

'She sinned,' Durrain went on, 'but it's wise to leave vengeance to the Forest.' She turned to Torak, and he felt the force of her gaze. 'You understand this now. It was something your mother always knew.'

Torak went still. 'My mother? But – you said you couldn't tell me anything about her.'

She gave him her thin smile. 'You were bent on revenge. You weren't ready to hear.' Tilting her head, she studied the shifting leaves above her. 'You were born in the Great Yew,' she said. 'When your mother felt her time come, she went to the sacred grove to seek the Forest's protection for her child. She went into the Great Yew. You were born there. She buried your navel-cord in its embrace. Then she and the Wolf Mage fled south. Later, when she knew her death was near, she sent him to find me, so she could tell the things she couldn't tell him.'

She held out her hand, and a spotted moth settled on her palm. 'The night you were born, the World Spirit came to her in a vision. He decreed that you must fight all your life to undo the evil which the Wolf Mage had helped create. She was frightened. She begged the World Spirit to help her child fulfil so hard a destiny. He said he would make you a spirit walker – but that you must then be clanless, for no clan should be so much stronger than the others.' She watched the moth flutter away. 'And he decreed that this gift must cost your mother her life.'

Torak stared at the leaf skeleton in his hands.

'To seal the pact, the World Spirit broke off a tine of his antler and gave it to her. She made it into a medicine horn. The day she finished it, she died.'

A redstart alighted on an alder, wiped its beak on the branch, and flew off.

'Your father,' said Durrain, 'left you in the wolf den and went to build her Death Platform. Three moons later, he brought her bones to the sacred grove and put them to rest in the Great Yew.'

Torak cast the leaf skeleton on the water and watched it carried away. The Great Yew. His birth tree. His mother's death tree.

He thought of his father, setting pegs in its ancient flanks to help his mate climb in when she was ready to give birth; then bringing back her bones and laying them to rest, along with her knife: the knife which, many summers later, had saved Renn's life.

On the other side of the river, a troop of ducklings followed their mother down the bank. Torak saw them without seeing them. He was clanless *because* he was a spirit walker. His mother had chosen to make him so, at the cost of her life.

A painful anger kindled within him. She could have lived, but she'd chosen to die. She had done it for him; but she'd left him behind.

Unsteadily, he got to his feet. 'I never wanted this.'

Durrain made to speak, but he motioned her back. 'I never *wanted* it!' he shouted.

Blindly, he ran through the Forest. He kept running till his thigh hurt too much to go on.

He found himself in a green glade netted with sunlight, where swallows swooped and butterflies flitted over windflowers. Beautiful, he thought.

And his dead would never see it.

As he sank to his knees in the grass, he thought of his mother and his father and Bale. The pain in his chest became as sharp as flint. For so long he had clung to his need for vengeance. Now it was gone, and there was nothing left but grief. A lump seemed to work loose under his breastbone, and he cried out. He went on crying: loud, heaving, jerky sobs. Crying for his dead, who had left him behind.

Renn lay in her sleeping-sack, staring into the dark. Her thoughts went hopelessly round and round. Fin-Kedinn had made her bow. Thiazzi had broken it. Fin-Kedinn was sick. The bow was an omen. Fin-Kedinn was dead.

Eventually, she could bear it no longer. Grabbing her crutches, she hobbled from the shelter.

It was middle-night, and the camp was quiet. She made her way to a fire and lowered herself onto a log, where she sat watching the sparks fly up to die in the sky.

Where was Torak? How could he do this? Running off

without telling her, when she was desperate to get back to the Open Forest.

Some time later, he limped into camp. He saw her and came to sit by her fire. He looked drained, and his eyelashes were spiky, as if he'd been crying. Renn hardened her heart. 'Where have you been?' she said accusingly.

He glowered at the fire. 'I want to get out of here. Back to the Open Forest.'

'Me too! If you hadn't gone off like that, we'd be on our way.'

With a stick he stabbed the embers. 'I hate being a spirit walker. It feels like a curse.'

'You are what you are,' she said unsympathetically. 'Besides, some good comes out of it.'

'What good? Tell me what good ever came out of it?'

She bridled. 'When you were a baby, in the wolf den. It's because you're a spirit walker that you learnt wolf talk. Which let you make friends with Wolf. There. That's good, isn't it?'

He went on glowering. 'But it's not just wolf talk, that's the thing. When you spirit walk – I think it leaves marks on your souls.'

Renn shivered. She'd been wondering about that, too. The rage of the ice bear, the viper's ruthlessness . . . At times, she saw traces of them in Torak. And yet – those green flecks in his eyes. Surely they were good: specks of the Forest's wisdom which had rubbed off on him, like moss off a branch.

But she was too annoyed to tell him about that now, so instead she said, 'Maybe it does leave marks, but not always. You spirit walked in a raven, and it didn't make you any cleverer.'

225

He laughed.

With her crutches, she pulled herself to her feet. 'Get some sleep. I want to leave as soon as it's light.'

He threw the stick into the fire and stood up. Then he reached behind him and put something into her hands. 'Here. I thought you'd want this.'

It was the pieces of her bow.

'Now you can lay it to rest,' he said. He sounded uncertain, as if he wasn't sure he'd done the right thing.

Renn couldn't trust herself to speak. As her fingers closed about the much-loved wood, she seemed to see Fin-Kedinn carving it. It *was* a sign. It had to be.

'Renn,' Torak said quietly. 'It's not an omen. Fin-Kedinn is strong. He will get better.'

She drew a breath that ended in a gulp. 'How did you know I thought that?'

'Well. I – know you.'

Renn pictured Torak limping through the Forest to retrieve the broken bow. She thought, Maybe spirit walking does leave marks. But this . . . this is simply Torak. 'Thank you,' she said.

'It wasn't much.'

'Not just for this. For what you did. For breaking your oath.' Putting her hand on his shoulder, she rose and kissed his jaw, then hobbled quickly away.

Wolf watched Tall Tailless blinking and swaying after the pack-sister had gone, and sensed that his feelings were as scattered and blown about as a flurry of leaves.

Taillesses were so complicated. Tall Tailless liked the pack-sister and she liked him, but instead of rubbing flanks and licking muzzles, they ran away from each other. It was extremely odd.

Thinking of this, Wolf trotted off to find Darkfur. She joined him, her muzzle still wet from the kill, and after play-biting and rubbing pelts, they ran together up-Wet. Wolf liked the feel of the cool ferns stroking his fur, and the patter of Darkfur's paws behind him. He snuffed the delicious smells of fresh fawn blood and friendly wolf.

The Forest was at peace again, and yet something made Wolf head for the place where Tall Tailless had fought the Bitten One. When they reached it, they slowed to a trot. The Bright White Eye gazed down upon the wakeful trees, and the dread of the Thunderer still floated in the air.

The Thunderer was a great mystery. When Wolf was a cub, the Thunderer had made him leave Tall Tailless and go to the Mountain. Later, when Wolf ran away, the Thunderer had been angry. Then Wolf was forgiven, although he wasn't allowed back on the Mountain. All this was very strange; but then, the Thunderer was male and female, hunter and prey. No wolf could understand such a creature.

Wolf used to *hate* not understanding, but now he knew that some things he just couldn't. The Thunderer was one, and Tall Tailless another. Tall Tailless was not wolf. And yet – he was Wolf's pack-brother. That was how it was.

A faint scent drifted past Wolf's nose, and he sprang alert. Darkfur's eyes gleamed. *Demons.*

Eagerly, Wolf put his muzzle to the ground, taking deep sniffs as he followed the trail. It led past the ancient trees and up the rise.

The Den was nearly blocked by a rock, the gap too narrow for Wolf to get in. He made it bigger by digging the earth with his forepaws, and Darkfur helped. At last,

Wolf squeezed through.

Inside, he caught a whiff of demon, but the scent was old. No demons here. Just a very thin, smelly tailless cub.

Wolf whined softly and licked her nose. She didn't even blink. Something was wrong. Wolf backed out of the Den and raced off to fetch Tall Tailless.

The Light had come when he drew near the Dens of the taillesses, and he saw at once that he would have to wait. On the edge of the Fast Wet, a group of floating hides had drawn up. Wolf watched the leader of the Raven pack climbing the bank, and the pack-sister throwing away her sticks and hopping towards him, and the pack leader laughing and swinging her into his forepaws.

THIRTY-NINE

'How long till we reach the Open Forest?' asked Torak.

Fin-Kedinn, rolling up his sleeping-sack, said, 'We should make it by dusk.'

'At last!' sighed Renn.

She tucked a scrap of dried boar in a birch for the guardian, but Rip promptly stole it. Torak tried to make his offering to the Forest raven-proof by stuffing it down a crack in an ash tree. Then Fin-Kedinn told Renn to put the fire back to sleep, and he and Torak carried the gear down to the canoes.

It was two days since they'd left the Deep Forest camp, and they were taking it slowly, as Fin-Kedinn's ribs were still mending. The Raven Leader had come alone, the rest of the clan being busy with the salmon run. It was good to be just the three of them.

Around him, Torak sensed a great healing. Even among the Deep Forest clans, there had been a coming together, sparked by the need to heal the stolen children. Five had been freed from holes dug into the slopes behind the sacred grove. All were stick-thin, their teeth filed to fangs, their minds scoured white as mistletoe berries. But after peering into their eyes, Renn had declared that Thiazzi hadn't yet trapped demons in their marrow, so they were still children, not tokoroths; and since she had more experience of this than anyone, even Durrain had deferred to her. The last Torak had seen of the Deep Forest clans, they'd been earnestly debating the best rites to aid the recovery.

The Forest, too, was beginning to overgrow its wounds. It had taken a day to paddle through the burnt lands, but in places, Torak had glimpsed patches of green, and a few hardy deer nibbling shoots. On the shores of Blackwater Lake, he'd seen the sacred mare. She'd whinnied at him, and he'd nickered back. It seemed that she'd forgiven him for riding her.

And yet, he thought as he stowed the waterskins in the canoes, some hurts would never heal. The Aurochs' scars would never fade. Gaup was maimed for life. His little girl, who'd been found with the others, was mute. Worst of all, one of the stolen children was lost for good. *Demon*, Wolf had said as he'd followed its trail, before losing it in the foothills of the Mountains. Torak pictured the tokoroth scuttling over the stones towards Eostra's lair.

'Better tie down the gear,' said Fin-Kedinn, making him jump. 'There's white water ahead.'

Torak was surprised; he didn't remember any rapids. Then he realized that he and Renn had made this part of the journey on foot, and south of the river. It was a relief to know that from now on, Fin-Kedinn was in charge.

They got under way, gliding past chattering alders and reed-beds alive with warblers. At last, as the light softened to gold, the Jaws of the Deep Forest loomed into view.

Over his shoulder, Fin-Kedinn asked Torak if he was sorry to be leaving the place where he was born.

'No,' said Torak, though it saddened him to admit it. 'I don't belong here. The Red Deer would've let the Oak Mage take over the Forest, rather than fight. And the others . . . They wanted to kill anyone who didn't follow the Way. Now I think they'd kill anyone who did. How can you trust people like that?'

Fin-Kedinn watched a swallow catch a fly on the wing. 'They need certainty, Torak. Like ivy clinging to an oak.'

'What about you? Do you need it?'

Fin-Kedinn rested his paddle across the boat and turned to face him. 'When I was young, I travelled to the Far North and hunted with the White Fox Clan. One night, we saw the lights in the sky, and I said, Look, there's the First Tree. The White Foxes laughed. They said, It's not a tree, it's the fires which our dead burn to keep warm. Later, when I was on Lake Axehead, the Otter Clan told me the lights are a great reed-bed which shelters the spirits of their ancestors.' He paused. 'Who's right?'

Torak shook his head.

Fin-Kedinn took up his paddle again. 'There is no certainty, Torak. Sooner or later, if you have the courage, you face that.'

Torak thought of the Aurochs and the Forest Horses, painting trees. 'I think some people never face it.'

'That's true. But not everyone in the Deep Forest is like them. Your mother wasn't. She had more courage.'

Torak put his hand to his medicine pouch. He hadn't yet told Fin-Kedinn what he'd learnt about the horn, but he had told Renn — and being Renn, she'd thought of something he hadn't. 'Maybe it's been helping you all the time. I always wondered why the Soul-Eaters never sensed that you're a spirit walker. And that humming noise at the sacred grove? Maybe it did bring the World Spirit. Though I don't think we'll ever know for sure.'

No certainty, thought Torak. The idea blew through him like a clean, cold wind.

As they swept into the shadow of the Jaws, he glanced back. The low sun glowed in the mossy spruce, and it seemed to him that they whispered farewell. He thought of the hidden valley where the Deep Forest clans had taken Thiazzi's corpse for secret funeral rites. He thought of the sacred grove where the great trees stood as they had stood for thousands of summers, watching the creatures of the Forest live out their brief, embattled lives. Did they care that he had broken his oath? Had they already forgotten?

It was not even a moon since Bale was killed, and yet it felt like a whole summer. Torak said to Fin-Kedinn, 'I promised to avenge him. But I couldn't do it.'

The Raven Leader turned and met his eyes. 'You broke your oath to save Renn,' he said. 'Don't you think that if things had been different – if you were the one who'd died, and he'd sworn to avenge you – don't you think he would have done the same?'

Torak opened his mouth, then shut it again. Fin-Kedinn was right. Bale would not have hesitated.

Fin-Kedinn said, 'You did well, Torak. I think his spirit will be at peace.'

Torak swallowed. As he watched his foster father deftly

plying his paddle, he felt a surge of love for him. He wanted to thank him for lifting such a load from his shoulders; for watching out for him; for being Fin-Kedinn. But the Raven Leader was busy steering their canoe around a submerged log and calling a warning to Renn in the other boat. Then they were out of the Jaws and into the Open Forest, and Renn was grinning and punching the air, and soon Torak was, too.

That night, as they camped by the Blackwater, Bale came to him for the last time.

Torak knows that he is dreaming, but he also knows that what's happening is true. He stands on the pebbly shore of the Bay of Seals, watching Bale carry his skinboat down to the Sea. Bale is strong and whole again, and he balances his skinboat on his shoulder with easy grace. When he reaches the shallows, he sets it on the water, jumps in and takes up his paddle.

Torak runs down to him, desperate to catch up, but already Bale is flying like a cormorant over the waves, leaving him behind.

Torak tries to call to him, but only manages a broken whisper. 'Wait!'

Out on the shining Sea, Bale brings his craft about.

'May the guardian swim with you!' cries Torak.

Bale waves his paddle in a glittering arc, and breaks into a grin. 'And run with you, kinsman!' he calls back.

Then he is off, his golden hair streaming behind him as he heads west, to where the sun is going to sleep in the Sea.

'Why *not*?' said Renn three moons later. 'You miss him. I do too. So let's go and find him.'

Torak didn't reply. He wore his stubborn look, and she knew it was no use suggesting that he should simply howl for Wolf. He wouldn't want to risk the disappointment, because these days, Wolf didn't often howl back. From time to time over the summer, he'd come to them, but although he was as affectionate and playful as ever, and had clearly got over his shock at Torak not being a wolf, at times, Renn sensed a distance in him, as if he were somewhere else. Torak didn't talk of it, but she knew that he felt it too, and that in his worst moments, he feared it meant the end of their old closeness.

So why doesn't he go and *find* him? she thought in exasperation. 'Torak,' she said out loud. 'You're the best tracker in the Forest. So. Track!'

She had to admit, though, it did feel odd to be tracking *Wolf*. But then, everything about this summer felt odd. She was still getting used to being a Mage, and although Saeunn remained the Clan Mage, people treated her even more warily than before.

Her gear, too, was unfamiliar: new medicine horn and pouch (this an unexpected gift from Durrain), new strike-fire, new axe, new knife. New bow. She'd laid the remains of her faithful friend in the Raven bone-ground, and the old Auroch man – who turned out to have known Fin-Kedinn in the past and taught him bow-making – had made her a splendid new one. It was of yew wood felled by the light of the waxing moon, and subtly fitted to her left-handed way of shooting. But she couldn't get used to it, and today she'd left it in camp; although she was beginning to worry that it might feel left out, so maybe next time she'd bring it along.

It was the Moon of Green Ashseed, and the willowherb stood shoulder-high. It was so hot that Rip and Rek flew with their beaks open to keep cool. It had been an unusually good summer, with plenty of prey and no-one dangerously ill. If Renn sometimes woke in the night from dreams of eagle owls and tokoroths, she soon went back to sleep.

She watched Torak stoop to examine a furrow where a wolf had scratched the earth after scent-marking. He sighed. 'It's not Wolf.'

Later, he picked a strand of black wolf hair off a juniper bush.

'Wolf has some black in his fur,' Renn said hopefully. 'In his tail and across the shoulders.'

'His hairs are only black at the tips,' said Torak. 'Not like this.'

For a long time after that, he went into what she called his tracking trance, following no sign that she could detect. Then he crouched so abruptly that she nearly fell over him.

By his knee, she made out the faintest shadow of a paw-print. 'Is it Wolf?' she whispered.

He nodded. His face was tense with hope, and Renn felt sorry for him, and cross with Wolf for not sensing that his pack-brother needed him.

But as they went on, she forgot her crossness and gathered some green hazelnuts as a present. The previous summer, Wolf had watched her forage in a hazel bush, then done the same, although he'd ignored the ripe ones and only crunched up the green.

She was thinking of that when a wolf howled in the next valley.

She stared at Torak. 'Wolf?' she mouthed.

He nodded. 'He's asking us to come to him.' He frowned. 'But I've never heard him make that call before.'

They reached the rise above the river, and suddenly Wolf was flattening Torak with a huge wolf welcome mixed up with a fervent apology. *I'm so happy you're here! Sorry, sorry, I missed you too! Happy! Sorry!*

Eventually he jumped off Torak and pounced on Renn to say it all over again, leaving Torak free to look about.

The space around the Den was littered with well-chewed scraps of bone and hide, the earth packed hard by many paws. Torak noticed that Wolf was thinner, probably because he'd had to do so much hunting. He began to smile. 'I should have guessed,' he murmured.

'Me too,' said Renn, pushing Wolf's nose away. Her eyes were shining, and she looked as happy as Torak felt.

A magnificent black she-wolf with green amber eyes emerged from the Den and trotted towards them, wagging her tail and sleeking back her ears in a diffident greeting.

Torak thought, Yes, of course. This is right.

Turning to Renn, he told her that the she-wolf had been part of the pack he'd befriended the previous summer. Together, they watched her lie down on her belly and sweep the earth with her tail, while Wolf disappeared into the Den.

'I think we should move back a bit,' said Torak, suddenly unsure how they should behave. He and Renn retreated a polite distance from the Den mouth, and sat cross-legged on the ground.

They didn't have long to wait. Wolf backed out, carrying a small, wriggling bundle in his jaws. Lashing his tail, he padded to Torak and set it before him.

Torak tried to smile, but his heart was too full.

The cub was about a moon old. It was fat and fluffy and not very steady on its short legs. Its ears were still crumpled, its eyes a slatey, unfocussed blue, but it wobbled eagerly towards Torak, as fearless and inquisitive as its father had been when he was a cub.

Torak whined softly and held out his hand for the cub to sniff, and it yipped and wagged its stubby tail and tried to eat his thumb. He scooped it up and nuzzled its belly. It batted him with small, neat paws, and snagged his hair with claws as fine as bramble thorns. When he set it down, it scampered back to its father.

The she-wolf raised her muzzle and whined, and two more cubs emerged from the Den and bounded towards her, mewing and nuzzling her jaws. One was black, with its mother's greenish eyes, while the other was grey, like Wolf, but with reddish-brown ears. All were trembling with excitement at this amazing new world.

Rip and Rek flew down, and two of the cubs fled, while their sister began to stalk. The ravens walked about, apparently unaware. They let the cubs prowl almost within reach, then flew off with raucous laughs.

Torak watched Renn lying on her side and dragging a stick for the cubs to chase, while – unknown to her – the black one sneaked up and gnawed her boots.

Torak glanced at Wolf, who stood proudly wagging his tail. *Thank you*, he said in wolf talk. Then to Renn, 'Do you realize what this means?'

She grinned. 'Well, I *think* it means Wolf has found a mate.'

He laughed. 'Yes, but it's more than that. This is the cubs' first time ever out of the Den. That's the most important day of all, because it's when they meet the rest of the pack.'

With a wave of his hand, he took in Wolf and his mate and the cubs, and Renn and himself. 'The rest of the pack,' he said again. 'That's us.'

AUTHOR'S NOTE

Torak's world is the world of six thousand years ago: after the Ice Age, but before the spread of farming to his part of north-west Europe, when the land was one vast Forest.

The people of Torak's world looked pretty much like you or me, but their way of life was very different. They didn't have writing, metals or the wheel, but they didn't need them. They were superb survivors. They knew all about the animals, trees, plants and rocks of the Forest. When they wanted something, they knew where to find it, or how to make it.

They lived in small clans, and many of them moved around a lot: some staying in camp for just a few days, like the Wolf Clan; others staying for a whole moon or a season, like the Raven and Willow Clans; while others stayed put all year round, like the Seal Clan. Thus some of the clans have moved since the events in *Outcast*, as you'll see from the amended map.

When I was researching *Oath Breaker*, I visited a number of the ancient trees with which the UK is so richly endowed. I also spent time in the largest area of primeval lowland forest left in Europe, in the Białowieża National Park in eastern Poland. There I saw the *żubroń* (a hybrid of cattle and European bison), boar, tarpan (a kind of wild horse), a number of lighting-struck trees, and more species of woodpecker than I'd ever seen. In Białowieża I gained inspiration for the various parts of the Deep Forest and its inhabitants, particularly during my long hikes into the Strictly Protected Area of the Forest. I also got the chance to study two magnificent beaver dams and lodges, which gave me the inspiration for Torak's hiding place.

Needless to say, I have also kept up my friendship with the wolves of the UK Wolf Conservation Trust. Watching the cubs grow to young adulthood and talking to their devoted volunteer carers has been a constant source of inspiration and encouragement.

I want to thank everyone at The UK Wolf Conservation Trust for letting me get close to their wonderful wolves; The Woodland Trust for helping me gain access to some of the ancient trees featured in my research; Mr Derrick Coyle, the Yeoman Ravenmaster of the Tower of London, whose extensive knowledge and experience of the ravens there has been a continual inspiration; the friendly and helpful people of the Authority of the Białowieża National Park and the Natural History and Forestry Museum at Białowieża; the guides of the Biuro Usług Przewodnickich Puszcza Białowieża and the PTTK Biuro Turystyczne, particularly the Rev. Mieczysław Piotrowski, Chief Guide of the PTTK, who – with the gracious permission of the Chief Forester of the Druszki district of the Białowieża National Forest – made it possible for me to see those beaver lodges.

Finally, and as always, I want to thank my agent, Peter Cox, for his tireless enthusiasm and support; and my truly gifted and altogether wonderful editor and publisher, Fiona Kennedy, for her imagination, commitment and understanding.

Michelle Paver
2008

Oath Breaker is the fifth book in the *Chronicles of Ancient Darkness*, which tell of Torak's adventures in the Forest and beyond, and of his quest to vanquish the Soul-Eaters. *Wolf Brother* is the first book, *Spirit Walker* the second, *Soul Eater* the third, and *Outcast* the fourth. The sixth and final book, *Ghost Hunter*, is also now available. Here is a preview of the first chapter.

ONE

Torak doesn't want to enter the silent camp.

The fire is dead. Fin-Kedinn's axe lies in the ashes. Renn's bow has been trodden into the mud. The only trace of Wolf is a scatter of paw-prints.

Axe, bow and prints are dusted with what looks like dirty snow. As Torak draws closer, grey moths rise in a swarm. Grimacing, he flicks them away. But as he moves off, they settle again to feed.

At the shelter, he halts. The doorpost feels sticky. He catches that sweet, cloying smell. He dare not go in.

It's dark in there, but he glimpses a heaving mass of grey moths – and beneath it, three still forms. His mind rejects what he sees, but his heart already knows.

He backs away. He falls. Darkness closes over him . . .

With a gasp, Torak sat up.

He was in the shelter, huddled in his sleeping-sack. His heart hammered against his ribs. His jaws ached from grinding his teeth. He had not been asleep. His muscles were taut with the strain of constant vigilance. But he had seen those bodies. It was as if Eostra had reached into his mind and twisted his thoughts.

It's what she wants you to see, he told himself. It isn't true. Here is Fin-Kedinn, asleep in the shelter. And Wolf and Darkfur and the cubs are safe at the resting place. And Renn is safe with the Boar Clan. *It isn't true.*

Something crawled along his collarbone. With a

shudder, he crushed it with his fist. The grey moth left a powdery smear and a taint of rottenness.

At the back of the shelter, another moth settled on Fin-Kedinn's parted lips.

Torak kicked off his sleeping-sack and crawled to his foster father. The moth rose, circled, and flitted out into the night.

Fin-Kedinn moaned in his sleep. Already, nightmares were seeping into his dreams. But Torak knew not to wake him. If he did, the evil images would haunt the Raven Leader for days.

Torak's own vision clung to him like the moths' unclean dust. Pulling on leggings, jerkin and boots, he left the shelter.

The Blackthorn Moon cast long blue shadows across the clearing. Around it, the breath of the Forest floated among the pines.

A few dogs raised their heads as Torak passed, but the camp was quiet. You had to know the Raven Clan as well as he did to perceive how wrong things were. The shelters huddled like frightened aurochs about the long-fire which burned through the night. Saeunn had ringed the clearing with smoking juniper brands mounted on stakes, in an attempt to ward off the moths.

In the fork of a birch tree, Rip and Rek roosted with their heads tucked under their wings. They slept peacefully. So far, the grey moths had only blighted people.

Ignoring the ravens' gurgling protests, Torak gathered them up and went to sit by the long-fire, his arms full of drowsy, feathered warmth.

In the Forest, a stag roared.

When he was little, Torak loved hearing the red deer

bellow on misty autumn nights. Snuggled in his sleeping-sack, he would gaze into the embers and imagine he saw tiny, fiery stags clashing antlers in fiery valleys. He'd felt safe, knowing that Fa would keep the dark and the demons away.

He knew better now. Three autumns ago, on a night such as this, he had crouched in the wreck of a shelter, and watched his father bleed his life away.

The stag fell silent. Trees creaked and groaned in their sleep. Torak wished someone would wake up.

He longed for Wolf, but howling for him would disturb the whole camp. And he couldn't face the long walk to find the pack.

How has it come to this? he wondered. I'm afraid to go into the Forest alone.

'This is how it starts,' Renn had told him half a moon before. 'She sends something small, which comes in the night. Something you can't keep out. And the grey moths are only the beginning. The fear will grow. That's what she feeds on. That's what makes her strong.'

Far away, an eagle owl called: oo-hu, oo-hu.

Torak grabbed a stick and jabbed savagely at the fire. He couldn't take much more of this. He was ready: he had a quiverful of arrows, and his fingertips ached from sewing his winter clothes. He'd ground the edges of his axe and knife so sharp they could split hairs.

If only he knew where to find her. But Eostra had hidden herself in her Mountain lair. Like a spider, she had cast her web across the Forest. Like a spider, she sensed the least tremor in its furthest strand. She knew he would hunt her. She wanted him to try. But not yet.

Scowling, Torak tried to lose himself in the glowing embers.

He woke to a voice calling his name.

The logs had collapsed. The ravens were back in their tree.

He hadn't dreamt that voice. He had heard it. It was familiar – unbearably so. It was also impossible.

Rising to his feet, Torak drew his knife. When he reached the ring of juniper brands that protected the camp, he paused. Then he squared his shoulders and walked past them into the Forest.

The moon was bright. The pines floated in a white sea of mist.

Above him on the slope, something edged out of sight.

Torak's breath came fast and shallow. He dared not follow. But he had to. He climbed, scratching his hands as he pushed through the undergrowth.

Halfway up, he stopped to listen. Nothing but the stealthy drip, drip of mist.

Something tickled his knife-hand.

At the base of his thumb, a grey moth fed on a bead of blood.

'Torak . . .' A pleading whisper from the trees.

Dread reached into Torak's chest and squeezed his heart. This wasn't possible.

He climbed higher.

Through the swirling mist, he glimpsed a tall figure standing by a boulder.

'Help me . . .' it breathed.

He blundered towards it.

It melted into the shadows.

It had left no tracks; only a branch, faintly swaying. But behind the boulder, Torak found the remains of a fire. The logs were cold, covered in ash. He stared at them. They'd been laid in a star pattern. This couldn't be. Only he and one other person built their fires that way.

Look behind you, Torak.

He spun round.

Two paces away, an arrow had been thrust into the earth.

Torak recognized the fletching at once. He knew the one who had made this arrow. He wanted desperately to touch it. He didn't dare.

He tried to lick his lips, but his mouth was dry.

'Is it you?' he called, his voice rough with fear and longing.

'Is it you? . . . *Fa*?'

CHRONICLES OF ANCIENT DARKNESS

Six adventures. One quest.

There are six books in the Chronicles of Ancient Darkness, and all feature Torak, Renn and Wolf.

In *Wolf Brother*, Torak finds himself alone in the Forest, when his father is killed by a demon-haunted bear. In his attempts to vanquish the bear, Torak makes two friends who will change his life: Renn, the girl from the Raven Clan, and Wolf, the orphaned wolf cub who will soon become Torak's beloved pack-brother.

In *Spirit Walker*, a horrible sickness attacks the clans, and Torak has to find the cure. His search takes him across the Sea to the islands of the Seal Clan, where he encounters demons and killer whales, and gets closer to uncovering the truth behind his father's death, as well as learning of his own undreamed-of powers.

In *Soul Eater* Wolf is taken by the enemy. To rescue him, Torak and Renn must journey to the Far North in the depths of winter, where they brave blizzards and ice bears, and venture into the very stronghold of the Soul-Eaters.

Outcast takes place on and around Lake Axehead. Torak is cast out of the clans, and has to survive on his own, separated from Renn, and even from Wolf.

In *Oath Breaker* one of Torak's closest friends is killed, and he tracks the murderer into the mysterious heart of the Deep Forest. Here the clans are at war, and punish any outsider venturing in. In the Deep Forest, Torak learns more about his mother, and about just why he is the spirit walker.

Ghost Hunter is the final adventure. Set in the High Mountains, it tells of Torak's battle against the most fearsome of all the Soul-Eaters, Eostra the Eagle Owl Mage, who seeks to rule both the living and the dead.

A legend for all time.